Murphy in the Underworld

Stories

by Jack Harte

THE GLENDALE PRESS

First published in Ireland by
THE GLENDALE PRESS
18 Sharavogue
Glenageary Road Upper
Dun Laoghaire
Co. Dublin, Ireland

Acknowledgements

Seven Stories (Profile Press); *Profiles 2* (Profile Press); *Reality; The Ulster Tatler; R.T.E. Radio; Pacific Quarterly, (New Zealand); Matrix Press; A New First English Course* (School and College Services); *The Connacht Tribune; "Es Tu"; "Es Tu '82"; Tracks; Sunday Independent (Story of the Month); The Journal of Irish Literature* (U.S.A.); The two illustrations in *Dunorlar's First Annual Festival of Satire* are by Henry J. Sharpe.

ISBN 0 907606 38 5

Cover by Steven Hope

Contents

Murphy in the Underworld   7

Come, Follow Me   16

In the Retirement Colony   24

His First Job   31

The Alchemist of Ballykillcash   40

Depths   50

The Thane of Cawdor Lives   55

The Bleeding Stone of Knockaculleen   62

Estrangement   70

Baptism of Water   77

Conquest   82

Dunorlar's First Annual Festival of Satire   88

The Land of Dwarfs   97

Gelding   120

Eternal Navvy   125

Queen B   128

Three for Oblivion   135

For Celia

Murphy In The Underworld

It came as a great surprise to Murphy to find that he could leave Hades at all. And to be able to leave once a year — that exceeded all expectation.

'Eternity revolves in a circular course, just as time follows the course of a spiral,' the lecturer explained in the acclimatisation class. 'But here in Hades there is no gradual realisation of the cycle; there are no flowers to blossom, no birds to migrate, no natural appetites to punctuate your existence. Change is unknown here: each revolution of the circle is a perfect repetition of the previous one. But between the old circle and the new one, between the dragon's tail and the dragon's mouth, there is an intermission. For this one night, November Night, the laws of eternity and infinity lapse, and you are free to return to the world of time and place for its duration.'

Murphy pondered long and luxuriously on his visit to the Upperworld. At first he thought of it only in a general way, as an escape from the grey monotony of the Caverns up to the blue sky and the green fields. Then his thoughts became more specific as he remembered the little village in the West of Ireland where he was born and reared, its cottages with their cobbled yards and a dung pit at every stable door, the bleak hills around the village straddled by meagre stone walls. It would be nice to see his mother again, He had not seen her for about ten years before he died, but he had written to her (and sent her a ten-pound note) every Christmas.

It would also be nice, he mused, to visit his mates in London, to have a stroll around the edge of Clapham Common, buy a packet of cigarettes in Oldtown, as was his custom, and drop down to the Alex. for a few pints. Except that he had no use for cigarettes and pints anymore!

Murphy wondered if it were possible to visit two places on the one night, or if he needed a special permit to do that. It was a pity he hadn't thought of asking the lecturer in the acclimatisation class. But it should be easy enough to get such information.

He enquired casually among the millions of souls that thronged the Caverns of Hades, but everyone he spoke to was apathetic and irritable; finally, someone suggested that he ask in the Information Office of the Administration Wing. Murphy didn't like the sound of that. The few times he had visited the Tax Office in London, his experiences had instilled in him an inclination to avoid such places at all costs. But, when further questioning of his fellow-souls had failed to enlighten him, Murphy decided, against all his better prejudice, to enter the Administration Wing. Besides, what else was there to do in Hades?

His first glimpse of the Administration Wing was an awesome sight. It was an extension off the Main Cavern of Hades. But what an extension! A long corridor stretched out into the distance, possibly into infinity, and off that corridor were thousands of smaller ones, each studded with doors to individual offices. It was truly a labyrinth of immense proportions. But everywhere was stamped the message that its purpose was not to baffle, but to serve.

There were signs and arrows, pointers and notices, all to assist in the efficient conduct of the business of Hades. Murphy studied the signs: 'First Applications', 'Registrations', 'Renewed Applications', 'Personnel', 'Private, Staff Only', 'Information'. That was his one! He followed the pointers for 'Information' down the Central Corridor, into a side-corridor, around several corners, and eventually arrived at a door with the sign in bold letters staring dauntingly at him.

He knocked timidly on the door. There was no reply. Perhaps they're gone to lunch, thought Murphy in relief. Then he remembered that there was no such thing as lunch in Hades. He opened the door cautiously. Inside was a long partition with a series of hatches built into it. A notice ordered: 'Ring bell for service.' Murphy rang the bell.

A hatch slammed open, reminding Murphy vaguely of a

confessional box. A sombre-looking soul peered out at him.

'I'm new here,' explained Murphy, 'and I wanted to get some information on the passes for November Night. You see, I'd like to visit two places that night, if I could. I'd like to go home to Ireland, but I'd also like to make the trip to London.'

'Have you filled in an application form?' boomed the voice through the hatch.

'No. Not yet,' replied Murphy.

'The first thing you must do is fill in an application form.'

'Righto. I'll do that. Thanks,' said Murphy, glad that that little matter had been disposed of so easily.

He made his way back to the Central Corridor and started looking for a sign, 'First Applications', which he had noticed earlier. Eventually he spotted it and followed carefully from one arrow to another until he arrived in a huge office with multitudes queuing at each hatch. Murphy took his place in one of the queues.

Progress towards the hatch was slow and tedious, but Murphy was preoccupied with his dreams of the Upperworld. He would visit Ireland first. It would probably be dusk when he got there, with the house-lights beginning to wink from the side of the mountain. His mother would be inside their cottage, pulling the curtains, heaping turf on the fire, wetting a pot of tea. She might not have heard of his death — there was no one who would have known to tell her. It would be nice if she thought he was still alive, because he was really; at least he didn't feel any different. And then he would travel down towards London through Dublin and Holyhead, past the slag heaps of Wales, just as if he were on the night train to Euston.

Eventually Murphy reached the top of the queue. He asked for an application form, explaining the peculiarity of his wishes.

The official shook his head. 'You're in the wrong office. You need to go to the "Special Applications" section and ask for Form D.23.'

Murphy felt frustrated, especially after spending so long in the queue. But there was no point in getting angry. So he trudged back to the Central Corridor and began searching again. A great weariness oppressed him. Then he realised: how could he feel weary when he had no body? It must be psychological, he concluded; everything was bloody-well psychological anymore.

After scouring the Central Corridor for a long while he saw a pointer for 'Special Applications', and after a further lengthy quest he discovered the office.

'I would like to fill in Form D.23,' Murphy intimated to the clerk behind the hatch, when he got to the top of that queue. 'You see, I would like to visit two places on November Night, my home in Ireland, and London where I used to work.'

'I'm afraid D.23 is not the correct form for you. This form is an application for spatial immunity. It's for someone who wants to visit no individual place, but the earth in general, covering all places at once. Now what you must do is this. You must go to "First Applications" and fill in two forms, one for each of the two places you wish to visit.'

So Murphy proceeded on his pilgrimage. A weak but indigenous voice inside him began to whisper that he should run, run until he was well clear of office and desk and clerk; but he silenced that voice ruthlessly, rivetting his thoughts to the little village on the shores of the Atlantic.

It was again a long tedious affair getting through the queue in the 'First Applications' section. But Murphy made it at last. 'I would like two forms to fill in, please,' said he to the clerk.

'Nobody gets two forms,' declared the clerk with a slow, deliberate and absolute shake of his head. Murphy gave up in despair.

When he emerged from the Administration Wing into the Main Cavern of Hades, he threw himself down dejectedly along the wall and sat brooding.

"It will be November Night shortly,' said a soul, who was sitting near him, more to himself than to Murphy.

'What!' exclaimed Murphy. 'It couldn't be!'

'It's as near as dam'it,' said the other.

'My God, the time flies down here,' gasped Murphy.

The other soul glanced at him curiously. 'Are you just over?' he asked.

Either he didn't understand the language in which Murphy phrased the subsequent remarks, or else they reached a level of obscenity which was far beneath his plumb, but he watched Murphy with the same curious expression as the latter stalked off muttering: 'No matter where you go, there's some bastard who got there before you and thinks he owns the shagging joint.'

Murphy had not gone far when he felt a transformation taking place. He suddenly sensed that the shackles were falling away, as if he were being released from all limitations. Instinctively he knew that he was free from Hades. It all came so naturally to him that it took him by surprise. He knew that one act of will was all that was required to take him to his mother's cottage in Ireland. He willed it, and he was there. His first thought on reaching the Upperworld was: 'What was all that bullshit about passes?'

* * *

The jurisdiction of Hades returned with the dawn. Murphy had not succeeded in getting to London. Not that he wasn't able! On the contrary, he experienced total freedom of movement. But when he got to his mother's cottage he found it dark and uninhabited. It looked as if nobody had lived there for years. But where could she be? He searched the neighbours' houses; he went around on all his relatives, eavesdropping on their conversations; but not a trace of her could he find anywhere. He searched vainly until morning when he felt the pull of Hades upon him again.

Could she have died? Surely someone would have told him. But then, who could have told him? He hadn't talked with anyone from home for many years; and, with the way he changed his digs every second week, his mother never knew his address. If she were dead, she would be here in Hades and he could find her.

Murphy looked about the Cavern. For the first time he realised the significance of the fact that souls had no distinguishing features as bodies had. Each looked exactly like the next; so any one of the souls in front of him could be his mother and he wouldn't know. He would have to speak to each of them to discover its identity. And Murphy had already found that souls were reluctant to talk at all. They were totally self-centred, brooding forever on their former lives.

There were countless millions of souls in Hades and to find his mother he would have to interview each one of them in turn. That would be an impossible task, even with all the time he had at his disposal (or, as he should say, even with all eternity at his disposal — he would have to stop using these 'temporalisms' as the lecturer called them; they gave him away as a newcomer).

'What about that vast Administration?' he thought. 'They must have some record of who comes in.'

But Murphy wasn't going to go through the same mill he had gone through before. He had often heard his mates in London claim that the best method of dealing with large offices was to ask for the man in charge. It was no use talking to the clerk: he tried to get rid of you; but ask for the man in charge and you had them all shitting in their trousers (that was another custom that became extinct on entering Hades!).

So he made his way to the Information Office again. He asked for the soul in charge and was ushered into a room which had the sign 'Superintendent' on the door.

Behind the desk sat the Superintendent who asked, without curiosity, what his problem was.

'It's like this,' began Murphy. 'On the night-off there I went back home. I was looking for my mother, but I couldn't find her anywhere. So I thought that maybe she was down here. I'm wondering if there is any way I can find out.'

'We do keep a record of all who are admitted,' replied the Superintendent. 'But unfortunately, due to shortage of staff, we have not yet been able to file the admission cards in any kind of order. If you wish you can go through the cards. However, it would probably be more advisable to search for herself. You see, even if you came across her card it would only confirm that she was here, it would be of no assistance in finding her.'

Murphy could not contain his irritation. 'What's the bloody use of this infernal Civil Service if you can't do something as simple as check if my mother is here? It's all bullshit as far as I can see. I spent the best part of a year queuing up to get a pass for November Night, and when the time came I found that I was able to go off without any pass at all.'

'You went to the Upperworld without a pass!' cried the Superintendent rising in horror off his seat. 'I see now that it's one of these anarchists I'm dealing with. Trying to destroy everything we have achieved! But you won't succeed, you won't succeed! Order will always triumph over the forces of disorder.'

'It's not much of an achievement, just to convince people they need something that they don't need at all. Any con-man could do that. So what are you making such a big deal out of it for?'

'The procedure of issuing passes for November Night is the basis of our whole Administration,' said the Superintendent, getting tensely emotional, 'and the Administration is the one thing which gives order and meaning to life in Hades. You anarchists will sneer at us; you will try to subvert our credibility. But we have succeeded in spite of you. Look at this wall-chart here. This is a blueprint for the future expansion of Hades. It is designed to cope with any possible increase in the rate of admission. Note that the Administration Corridor is going to replace the Main Cavern as the focal point of the Underworld. See how all future developments are going to radiate from the Administration Corridor in a grid pattern. That's what order and progress are about. That's what you're undermining when you go to the Upperworld without a pass.'

'As far as I'm concerned you can stick your order and progress up your —' Murphy checked himself against the use of a temporalism. 'Since there's nothing you can do for me I'll go and start searching for my mother.' Murphy moved towards the door.

'The rules are that you cannot go around annoying souls in any of the main Caverns or in the new sections,' said the Superintendent, coming after him.

'Where am I supposed to look then?' asked Murphy angrily.

'The Lost Souls' Section,' replied the Superintendent. 'It's a designated area of Old Hades. It may be a comfort to you,' he put as much sarcasm as he could into these words, 'to know that about ninety percent of your nation is down there already. Along with other undesirable qualities, they bring their ghetto-mentality with them.'

For the first time since he entered Hades, Murphy experienced something approaching joy. The idea of an Irish settlement in the Underworld warmed him to the core. He couldn't wait to find it.

He hurried back to the Main Cavern and proceeded in the direction of Old Hades. When he had travelled a distance he noticed that the throngs were getting thinner and thinner. Eventually he heard a hum in the distance, a low steady hum. The further he went, the louder the hum became, until it reached a deafening intensity. Then, rounding a corner he saw, stretched out before him, the Lost Souls' Section of Hades.

There were myriads of souls, mingling restlessly, crying out in loud voices, shouting names, asking questions, millions of them in perpetual motion like water-beads in a turbulent seething ocean.

Murphy gazed at this pitiable sight. 'Finding someone in that melee,' he thought, 'must be at greater odds than winning the pools.' He saw, within the swirl, two souls meet, identify, embrace, cling to each other lest they should be separated by the next swell and be lost again for all eternity. But for the two that met there were millions who were still searching.

Perhaps his mother wasn't there at all. She might have chosen to remain in the relative peace of the other Caverns. For all he knew, she mightn't even be dead yet. Wouldn't he be a right mug if he was going around screaming her name in this infernal din, and she still up above, drinking a bottle of stout, maybe.

But what else was there to do? He listened intently to the babble. He could distinguish many shades of Irish dialect from Dublin to Donegal, from Kerry to Sligo, interspersed with an occasional phrase uttered in a strange language. And far away, Murphy could swear he heard someone singing in a drunken drawl.

> *Come back, Paddy Reilly, to Ballyjamesduff,*
> *Come home, Paddy Reilly, to me.*

He remembered all the people from home who had died; they would all be in there; so would all the men he had worked with in England. Even if he didn't find his mother, he might meet someone he knew; and even if he didn't meet anyone he knew, he would surely have the odd good chat.

So Murphy plunged into that sea of restless souls and began shouting and questioning like the rest of them. Then he was suddenly arrested by a curious thought; he wondered whether this was heaven or hell. But a moment's reflection convinced him of the irrelevance of that question, and he resumed calling out his mother's name among the lost souls of Hades.

Come Follow Me

Bonaparte Lane was a back street in our neighbourhood off the great thoroughfare of Bonaparte Avenue. It is a rundown deserted place now, but when I was ten years old it housed a lively community of a dozen families or more. Few streets, or families, experience the finality of a 'Last Day', but on one dark evening in November Bonaparte Lane ceased to exist as a community.

I witnessed that climax, that catastrophe, so I feel I am better qualified than most to chronicle the events which caused it.

Bonaparte Lane had a reputation of legendary proportion all over our city for the excellence of card-playing that could be witnessed nightly in all its houses. The best players from every quarter of the city would converge on the little lane to try their skills and their intelligence against the citizens of this revered street. For someone who was learning the art of card-playing, it was a big moment in his life when he felt ready for his first visit to so awe-inspiring an arena. Fathers, around the family card-table, would encourage their young sons by saying: 'You'll soon be fit for Bonaparte Lane.' Or, if any slovenly play was detected at a card-game in a distant quarter of the city someone might comment: 'If they had you in Bonaparte Lane, they'd throw you in the river' — a reference to the woefully polluted stream that intersected the Lane at the bottom end.

But slovenly play was never tolerated at the card-tables in the Lane. If anyone were found to be cheating or trying to cheat, play would cease immediately, and the offender would be asked to leave the house; a person thus disgraced would not be permitted to sit down to a card-table in Bona-

16

parte Lane for the rest of his life.

Gambling was outlawed as ruthlessly as cheating and there was never so much as a penny staked on any game in the Lane. There were those who thought this policy short-sighted, because the men, women and children of the street were brilliantly skillful at cards and if they took to playing for stakes they could have reduced the rest of the city to beggary.

Tradition was deeply rooted in the little community. The ethics and standards governing their card-playing were handed down to them along with the skills over many generations. And so they regarded themselves as the custodians of these ethics and these skills, singled out as a kind of chosen people, a race apart. Saturday nights were reserved for playing exclusively among themselves; but often outsiders came just to watch these games and to observe card-playing at its very best.

One day — it was either in the late spring or early summer — a sailor staggered into the entry and asked the children playing there where the 'casino' was. Naturally enough, they stared at the intoxicated seaman uncomprehendingly. Quickly recognising their confusion, he took a pack of cards out of his pocket and brandished them wildly over his head.

'Where do they play cards?' he asked in the rhythmless voice of one who has had to learn the language.

The children's faces lit up on recognising the familiar object.

'In every house,' came their chorus of reply.

'Which is the best house?' asked the sailor.

The children were again perplexed. They looked around and saw me standing a short distance away. I was a little older than they, so they looked pleadingly to me to resolve the problem. The way I reasoned it, one house was as good as the next, but the only house in which he would be welcome at that hour of the day was Alex Bryce's. Alex lived alone and spent most of the day in bed or lounging about, so he was always happy to have someone call in. I directed the sailor towards Alex's house, and watched him totter down the footpath and disappear through the perennially open door.

Bonaparte Lane was never the same again. The sailor turned out to be not only gifted as a player but also adept at every type of game. Heretofore, different individuals were champions and undisputed masters of certain games; but within a week the sailor had challenged and defeated each master at his own game. The citizens of the Lane rallied against this threat to their supremacy. All day and all evening they plotted and devised strategies; all night they pitted their knowledge and cunning against the foreign sailor in game after game. But the sailor disposed of each challenge with the ease and competency of one who was merely engaging in some preliminary exercises. When it finally became evident that he was never going to be beaten, a depression set in over the whole community. People gathered, as if by force of custom, at their usual rendezvous points but no one was interested in playing cards. It was not the fact of being beaten that disheartened the people — they had often experienced defeat before, on an individual basis — it was the fact that one man could take on the whole Lane, with its wealth of expertise, and win. It shook their confidence. It raised a question mark over their faith in the superiority conferred on them by tradition.

The sailor had taken up lodgings in Alex Bryce's and seemed in no hurry to return to the sea. When the visitors at night declined his invitation to play cards he grew morose and sent for whiskey. While he swallowed the liquor straight from the bottle he shuffled the pack of cards and dealt them out in various patterns, muttering to himself in his own language.

Then one night, when the visitors arrived, they found the sailor sober and excited. He had the table pulled into the middle of the floor and set ready for a card-game.

'Sit down! Sit down!' cried he. 'And I will teach you some new games. I have many games that I learned in Rio De Janeiro, and Port Said, and Casablanca.'

They reluctantly took their seats. The sailor deftly shuffled the pack and flicked the cards to all who were seated.

'This game is called "Cinch"', said he, and proceeded to outline the rules of the game. The visitors warmed to the idea of learning a new game and quickly mastered it. Then the sailor went on to instruct them in 'Fan Tan'.

The following night almost everyone from the Lane crowded into Alex Bryce's house to learn the new games from the sailor. They were enthusiastic about some of the games which demanded skill, intelligence, concentration; but they were apathetic about others which demanded nothing of the player but proceeded mechanically toward an outcome determined by haphazard luck.

The sailor had a vast repertoire of card-games and after three weeks he was still demonstrating new ones.

Then one night, while interest was still high, he asked loudly: 'Can anyone read the cards?:

An instantaneous silence descended on the room. The people of Bonaparte Lane were very wary of that aspect of cards and never dabbled in it, either in earnest or in fun.

'Come, come, it is only another game,' enticed the sailor. 'Cut the cards and we will find out which of the ladies dreams of a lover. The secrets of the mind revealed! Who will cut the cards?'

He started to shuffle the pack. A woman at the door coughed, muttered a goodnight, and made her way out. She was followed by another, and soon all the women were leaving, herding their youngsters in front of them.

But the men stayed, and it evidently proved to be the most engaging of all demonstrations because not one of them stirred out of the house until three in the morning. And the following evening, as they ate a hurried dinner, the men were full of wonder and admiration and excitement.

Because I was only a child then I heard little of what was going on at the sailor's card-table during the following nights. All discussion about it among the adults was carried on in huddled groups. The women were anxious and edgey and were in no humour for casual conversations with a youngster from a neighbouring street.

The days went by and the men became more reticent and more involved. Often they stayed at cards so late that some of them were not able to rise for work the following morning. Eventually one man stopped going to work altogether, then another, until finally there wasn't a man in the whole Lane who was holding a regular job. This left them free to start into the cards as soon as they cleared the sleep out of their eyes and had eaten whatever meagre breakfast was provided by their disaffected wives.

The strongest protest against what was happening in Bonaparte Lane was made by the priest. Some said he recognised the Devil's handiwork when he heard of the card-playing; others held that he had nearly exploded when he found a 'nil' return from the Lane in the Church collection. He appeared in the entry one day fully robed as if he were going to say Mass, walked down the Lane, and stopped outside Alex Bryce's. He took out his breviary and started to recite prayers in an incomprehensible murmur. Every now and again he would raise his right hand in a gesture towards the sky. He spent at least half-an-hour in the middle of the street, watched by three or four women, a lot of curious children, and a few dogs, and when he had finished he departed as enigmatically as he had come, without a word of explanation. Some held the opinion that he was putting his curse on the house; one woman suggested that he might have been praying for the souls of the men within, but she was contradicted flatly by the rest who declared that, whatever he was doing, his tone was not appropriate to praying. There was no indication from the house that the men were aware of the incident in the street outside; at least if they were so aware they did not stop play even to look out the window.

Gradually a severe poverty began to afflict the families in the Lane. Objects of value were pawned to put food on the table. The tyres of the car outside Murnaghan's went flat, the chassis rusted, and the engine seized; what had been a family car was now a derelict. The rounds of the St. Vincent De Paul man took on a major importance in the life of this formerly prosperous little street.

One evening around tea-time I was sitting underneath Newmans' window. I happened to overhear part of an argument between Martin Newman and his wife. It was the only hint I ever got of what was going on at Alex Bryce's card-table, and even that hint wasn't very enlightening.

'Where is it all leading to?' asked Mrs. Newman in a slightly demented tone. 'What do you expect to find out?'

'It's not what you find out at the end of the journey that's important,' replied Martin. 'It's what you learn along the

Come, Follow Me 21

way. The cards represent the whole world. Right? When they're laid out in different patterns and different combinations, it's amazing how much they tell you about life. Yet, no matter how much you learn, you feel you are about to understand something far more important. Only it keeps eluding you like the horizon or the rainbow's end.'

'Your family is on the brink of starvation. You have no job, nor the prospect of one. And you want to learn about life from a pack of cards. It's above in the asylum the lot of you should be.'

'Will you hold your tongue, woman,' shouted Martin. 'There are higher things in life than jobs and food. But you wouldn't appreciate that. Would you?'

A moment later he almost tripped over my legs in his haste down the street towards Alex Bryce's.

As the winter crept in and the weather became harder the predicament of the families worsened rapidly. Without fuel the houses were cold and damp. A flu epidemic had most of the children confined to bed. It was at that time that the women of the Lane gathered into Pearse's house where a year-old infant was ill with the flu. John Pearse, along with the other men, had already settled into the cards over in Bryce's house. His wife was nearly distracted with worry about the infant, and the other women were consoling her.

'When John comes home, you have a good chat with him,' said Mrs. Hynes. 'He's a good man, and when he sees how worried you are about the child he'll do something.'

'You're a silly woman, Mary Hynes,' declared Mrs. Newman. 'You don't understand. None of you does. You think that this is going to be over soon. You think that someday you'll wake up and it will all be behind you, like a bad nightmare. Well you're wrong. It will never be over. Never, I said. The men have gone their own way, searching for something. Mind you, they don't know what they're looking for, so I suppose they wouldn't recognise it even if they found it. But they have forgotten about their responsibilities. They no longer feel any obligations to us or to the children. I can see from your faces that you don't believe me. Or maybe you don't want to believe me but that a voice inside you is whispering that I'm right. And I'll prove I'm right. Do you all agree that John Pearse was as good and as kind a man as ever walked down Bonaparte Lane?'

There was a general nodding of assent.

'Mollie,' she said gently to Mrs. Pearse. 'Can I have your permission to send a message over to John to say that the baby is dying and that he had better come quickly. Now if he refuses to come on a summons like that, and I think he will refuse, it will prove my point.'

Mrs. Pearse nodded slowly and bit on her lower lip.

Mrs. Newman turned around and eyed me standing just inside the door.

'Cornelius,' she called. 'You bring the message over to John Pearse. Tell him that his baby is dying and that he is needed urgently at home. Tell him that, and tell him nothing more.'

I didn't like the job I was given, but such was the atmosphere in the house that I didn't even contemplate refusing. I went outside and crossed the street. The place was deserted and so quiet I imagined the tapping of my crutches echoed from one end of the Lane to the other. Up the three granite steps I advanced tremulously. The door to the living room opened without a creak, and I stepped into the preoccupied silence within. Momentarily I stood unnoticed inside the door. The sailor was sitting at the centre of the table and the rest of the men were gathered around it, like those pictures of Christ and his disciples at the Last Supper.

Then Alex Bryce looked up from the table and noticed me. The others turned around.

'Well, Cornelius,' said Alex. 'What are you doing here?:

'I have a message for John Pearse,' said I. 'His baby is dying and he's wanted at home.' I blurted out my message abruptly and noticed the immediate impression of shock it created on the men's faces. Silent, motionless, they stared one at another. It was as if a moment they had long awaited had finally arrived.

No one replied to me, so I withdrew from the room and made my way back across the empty street. Inside Pearse's front door again I opened my mouth to report the completion of my mission, but it was obvious from the faces there that I didn't have to say anything. They were waiting now.

The silence in that living-room was deathly, but very real, palpable. All the women stared fixedly at something in front of them, the corner of the table, the flame of the Sacred Heart lamp, or the empty fire-grate.

The children could be heard coughing in the bedroom upstairs. In the distance the lonely sound of a ship's horn hooted out over the city. Seconds plodded by as if they were retarded with weights of lead.

There was no sign of activity in the house across the street. Not a curtain flickered; not a shadow darkened the open door.

After half-an-hour Mrs. Newman broke the silence. 'We'll give him until ten-past-eight. That's a full hour from the time we sent the message.'

Nobody else opened a mouth, and the utter silence re-enveloped the room. Minute followed agonising minute.

Mrs. Pearse began to weep quietly and Mrs. Newman put an arm around her shoulders. But no one else moved. They were too preoccupied with their own pain. For they recognised that this was their tragedy as well as Mrs. Pearse's. If her husband would not come to her on such an awesome bidding, then no husband would answer any summons.

As soon as the clock turned ten-past-eight, the women shook themselves and began to get up quietly, as if a hypnotist had clicked his fingers to waken them from a trance. There was a clarity about them also, a suggestion that they were confronting a harsh reality with cold awareness, a feeling that the trance and the dream had been absolutely dispelled.

They each left without saying a word, and proceeded to their own houses. There they gathered together their children, blankets, clothes, and whatever food they had. And each woman left her home, turned her back on Bonaparte Lane, and set out for some other quarter of the city. By midnight there wasn't a woman or child left in the Lane.

I saw very few of them afterwards. Some went to their parents, some to relatives, some to institutions of one kind or another. But none of them ever returned to their homes in Bonaparte Lane.

In The Retirement Colony

On his retirement from the position of senior architect in the Building Corporation, Albert Maloney was dispatched with his wife and chattels to the Grade 1 Resort of K- on the South-East Coast. In tribute to the position he had attained on the occupational scale, he was given a detached house (no. 9830) with a modest garden front and rear.

The agent who met them and introduced them to their new home stressed the quietness of the neighbourhood, the short walk to the seafront, the proximity of amenities, and the remove of the Grade 2 Resort. But Albert noted, with satisfaction, how little the surroundings differed from the suburbs they had left; there were rows of secluded houses, each with its neatly-kept rose garden. He could not fault the house he was given either; it was more than adequate. Houses were allotted according to rank, and the allotment did not take into account the needs of the occupants. So, according to the order of things, Albert and his wife found themselves with a five-bedroom house.

On the following day they were visited by two members of the Residents' Committee who welcomed them to the resort and described the whole range of pastimes and sports that was open to them. They then brought Albert and his wife outside and introduced them to Mr and Mrs 9829 and Mr and Mrs 9831.

It was a smooth transition and Albert was soon settled into a routine of bowling in the morning, a little golf in the afternoon, a walk along the seafront in the evening with Mrs Albert followed by a few drinks at the club. His wife quickly became assimilated into the life of the Retirement Colony likewise: she became involved in a round of coffee mornings,

24

and (in the absence of charity committees to work for) the ladies knitted and sewed items of dress for each other.

In accordance with the rationale of the Great Plan, people enjoyed the quality of retirement they had earned as workers. And Albert had worked hard. For forty years he had sat before a drawing-board designing public toilets, council houses, recreation centres, libraries, office blocks; for forty years he had driven to the office in the early morning and driven home from the office in the late evening; for forty years he had watched television five nights a week and indulged in gentle social intercourse at the weekends. For forty years he had held before his mind the prospect of a luxury retirement in a Grade 1 Resort. And his life had been a total success.

Albert had no interest in gardening, but his wife thought that he ought to cultivate a rose-bed or, at least, keep the hedges trim. All the other husbands took pride in their gardens and Mrs Albert did not wish to be embarrassed before her friends. So she asked the horticultural adviser to call on Albert. Twice the adviser called but found no one at home. The next time he called, he caught Albert making an earlier-than-usual expedition to the bowling green.

Albert cursed his luck, in his own quiet way, but listened respectfully to the adviser's monologue on soil nutrition, environmental improvement, rotation of crops, etc., etc.; but all he could remember, when the adviser had gone, was: 'What you need is topsoil, plenty of topsoil.' That encounter left Albert depressed all day. He felt he was now obliged to make some token effort. Back in the city he had always hired a casual gardener one day each fortnight to take care of his hedge and lawn. But that wasn't possible here; here everyone was retired, and all the retired workmen were over in the Grade 2 Resort.

Day followed day, and Albert soon forgot about the garden and the horticultural adviser. It was more difficult to induce oblivion to the ever-present stimulus of his wife's nagging; but he was so content with his pastimes that no care could occupy the vacancy of his mind for very long.

His retirement stretched out before Albert like a placid ocean which is almost too indolent to reflect the sun. But the placidity of the ocean is convulsed by the onslaught of a sudden storm. And the peace of Albert's life was similarly rocked by something as inconsequential as a dream.

It was not an exceptional dream. With his father and brothers he was building a pyramid, not even an ornate pyramid — like the ones in Guatemala — just a regular Egyptian-style pyramid. They were constructing it from cut limestone, carrying each block on a litter up a steep ramp. Working, and sweating, and grunting, they lodged stone upon stone and the pyramid was very close to completion. It was a gigantic structure and each time they descended to the ground for another block, they paused to look up at it with silent pride.

That was the full extent of the dream but it left Albert's mind in a state of intense agitation. Childhood memories and obscure longings arose from remote corners of his soul. He remembered his father building a shed at the back of their house in the long twilit evenings of a distant summer. He remembered his brothers picking potatoes when November frost had stiffened the clay. He remembered the delicious sweat that lathered his face when they were working furiously at the hay to rescue it from the weather.

The morning after his dream Albert lay in bed for a long while. The time for his bowling came and went. The time for his lunch passed. The time for his trip to the golf course arrived, but Albert continued to lie in bed, remembering. It was evening when he eventually arose, much to the relief of Mrs Albert who had been contemplating summoning a doctor. But he went around the house in an air of remoteness as if he had lost touch with his surroundings.

The pyramid that he and his family had built preoccupied Albert for many days thereafter. He forgot about his bowling and his golf, and stayed indoors meditating the structure, mentally gauging stress and thrust. Eventually he took down his drawing-board and began to make sketches of the pyramid as he remembered it. When the sketches were finished he started detailed drawings based on his own experience and knowledge of architecture.

Day after day Albert remained indoors poring over his drawings, and the more he progressed, the more he marvelled at the ingenuity of the ancient builders. Sometimes they situated a pyramid to encompass a hill; it cut down on filling; and their calculations could be trusted to produce total symmetry in the end. What labour to lay that solid square! What thousands of slaves it took to lift it from the earth! With what indignation the captive tribes of Israel raised those soaring triangles! Soaring towards what? Towards the apex and the centre! Towards unity and perfection! Towards a monumental image of life and a symbol of death!

Mrs Albert's anxiety was fanned to panic by her husband's strange behaviour. He had never before acted in an unpredictable way. Without doubt he was unwell; yet he would not admit her to the room to ascertain his temperature; nor would he accept his customary mild laxative. She invited some of his friends from the golf club to come and speak to him, but they tapped fruitlessly on the room door.

How glorious for an architect to design and construct a building which trenscends the mundane, the trivial! What a waste was his own life, thought Albert. The dream revealed it all. He should have worked with his own people. Triangle over square! Together they could have raised a monumental image of life, a symbol of death.

Albert cursed the order of things that had decreed his separation from his people. One house, one shed built out of that relationship would have been worth more than all the office blocks and libraries he had ever designed. Now it was too late. Now he was in the Grade 1 Resort enjoying the quality of retirement he had earned as a senior official of the Building Corporation.

Disillusion and depression became intense. Albert's only joy now was his reveries of childhood. They were always memories of work, but work performed in an emotional environment. That was what was lacking in his life since then — an emotional environment. He longed to be re-united with his family; he longed for the security of his father's affection, his brothers' prowess; he longed to perform even one act in communion with them. But they were all in the Grade 2 Resort.

Albert started walking abroad again, taking a particular interest in the monstrous dividing wall between the Grade 1 Resort and the Grade 2 Resort. He studied the rows of spikes which continued the division out into the sea. When he swam out from shore he saw the overcrowded beach on the other side of the wall; there were thousands of people hustling and jostling for room; cheap food vendors' stalls lined the short untidy promenade. When he climbed the hill beyond the rows of houses he could see over the wall; he saw the high-rise flats which might have been constructed from one of his own blueprints; he saw the people going to-and-fro on the open landings in unbelievable numbers; he saw the paltry courtyards which seemed to be the only amenity areas in the whole scheme.

Conditions in the Grade 2 Resort were obviously deplorable. Two weeks previously Albert would have been repelled by the sight or even the thought of such squalor. Now, because of his dream, he felt differently. A strong feeling of affinity with this bustling mass had established itself firmly in his heart.

It was not possible to travel from the Grade 1 Resort to the Grade 2 Resort, Albert was informed by the estate agent, the only official he could find in the whole Retirement Colony. But Albert was determined to visit the Grade 2 Resort nevertheless. So he would have to go under it. A tunnel — from his back garden — topsoil, plenty of topsoil. His course was settled: he would drive a tunnel from his own garden, from inside his garden shed, under the dividing wall and into the Grade 2 Resort.

Mrs Albert was greatly relieved on seeing her husband out-and about again, and she resumed her daily routine. She was even more pleased when she heard that he was going to start gardening.

Albert surveyed the route the tunnel would take, and from his vantage point on top of the hill he planned exactly where he would surface on the other side of the wall. On the pretext that he was going to start digging the garden and repairing the garden shed, he purchased a pick, spade, shovel, crow-bar, sledge-hammer, saw and timber beams.

Before he could begin to tunnel he had to dig the garden, so that he could spread out the excavated soil. Then he started to sink a vertical shaft from inside the shed. He had no fear of discovery as his wife never came into the garden. She fluttered her fingers at him whenever she was passing between the front door and the gate. Once, she paused to enquire what type of flower he was planting, but she was quite content when she could chatter securely to her friends about her husband's newly-found passion for gardening.

When his wife was away from home in the morning and in the afternoon, Albert worked on the tunnel; when she was at home he barrowed the clay from the shed into the garden and spread it out over the ground.

His hands blistered and hurt at first, but he didn't mind; he welcomed the appearance of brown welts at the base of his fingers, the disappearance of some of the soft pink flesh. What absence of personality those hands showed! Even his face — and Albert touched the skin that hung limply from his jawbones — showed no qualities of character. He was glad he had no children: he could never have left an impression on them, as adults had left on him when he was a child. He remembered an old uncle who used to smoke a pipe — he would rummage in his pocket and bring forth a crumpled matchbox smelling of sweat — his uncle's matchbox had more personality than had Albert's face. But now he was digging his way to those real people. He would start again. He would work and build. And that thought lent force to his pick.

On the rafters of the shed he fixed a pulley and used it to raise the bucket of clay to the surface. When he had reached a depth of fifteen feet he began to cut the horizontal shaft. He had to be careful now as the earth was soft. Every five feet he placed a pair of timber props and ran flat bars from one prop to another to support the weight of the roof. Progress was slow but Albert was in no hurry. He relished every hour he spent in the tunnel. It was the greatest undertaking of his life.

One afternoon the horticultural adviser was passing and he stopped when he saw Albert. He looked at the extra soil spread out over the garden and was visibly shocked. He scratched his forehead with rapid motions of his fingers and enquired where Albert got the soil. The reply was couched in the vaguest possible terms. 'You've been fleeced. That's not topsoil, that's the poorest quality subsoil. You wouldn't grow moss on that.' And Albert assured him that he would pursue the matter with his supplier and demand compensation.

It was a cause of great exultation when, according to his calculations, he had driven his tunnel under the dividing wall. The awareness that fifteen feet above him were his family and perhaps the vast majority of the people he had known as a child rippled gaily through his mind. Even the clay seemed warmer.

In the next few days he worked harder than before and soon reached the point where he was to ascend.

At ten o'clock on a Monday morning Albert commenced cutting the vertical exit shaft. Dumping the buckets of clay was a slow operation at this stage, but he estimated that the exit would be complete by the end of the week.

About an hour after he had started he heard a loud thud. Stunned by the shock of anticipated disaster, he crept back through the tunnel to find that there had been an extensive cave-in. The props had collapsed under the weight of the roof. It was just beneath the dividing wall. He had under-estimated the pressure of the wall.

Albert started shovelling away the fall-in. He had to clear a vent quickly or he would suffocate. For an hour he worked frantically but did not succeed in breaking through. When his breath came in deep jerking gasps he knew the air was used up. He threw aside the shovel and lay down. The heavy breathing was tearing at his lungs. Exhausted, he closed his eyes. Beads of sweat were running down his forehead. He looked around and saw that his father's brow also was lathered in sweat and that he too was panting under the great weight of the stone, which was placed closer to his end of the litter. They strained and stumbled up the ramp, higher and higher. Despite their fatigue they were proud and full with a sense of purpose, for this was the final block of the pyramid, the coping-stone, the apex, and the centre.

His First Job

Michael was three weeks working for the Turf Company when the ganger announced that they were all to go footing turf the following day. It was no surprise, for they had been watching the neat rows of sods drying in the June sunshine; each day, as they crossed the flat expanse of turf spread out on the bank, the men would stoop to lift a sod and note the hardening crust on the exposed surface.

It was curious to Michael that although the men talked about the money they would earn, working at piece-rate on the footing, there seemed to be little joy in their voices. Michael himself was looking forward to the footing, for he was determined to save money that summer. He was on holidays from school and since he was over sixteen he was entitled to get his employment cards and take a job on the bog. The following year he would finish school and, if he got a scholarship, would go to the University. He would need a lot of money.

'Come on, lad, are you getting tired?' Jim O'Donnell called to him and doubled back to help him finish his piece.

They were tidying a clamp of turf that stretched from one end of the bog to the other, a distance of five miles. There were six of them on the job, all seasoned labourers except for Michael, and they had covered about a mile since he had joined them.

The other men were finished their strips and were standing, waiting. They were very helpful and treated him with a fatherly concern, sometimes sending him on an errand when they thought he was growing tired.

'We'll take one more strip each and then we'll go for the dinner,' said Christy O'Brien. 'It's the last time we'll be paid

31

for sitting down, so we may as well make the most of it.'

They paced the side of the clamp and took another five yards each. This time Michael did not pause: he gathered up the sods that were scattered at the base and threw them up on top of the clamp. When he had tightened up the base he arranged the sods on the side, sloping them from top to bottom so that the rain would not penetrate into the clamp. It was a job that was usually done in the autumn after the turf was collected, but, as the men explained, the Company had been short of money and could not afford to keep the usual quota of labourers over the previous autumn and winter; as a result jobs like this had been neglected.

This time they finished simultaneously. They had to walk back where they had started in the morning to collect their coats and bags. Before them the clamp on which they had toiled stretched out to the horizon where it converged with the two wide turf banks and the trench between them; even the parallel clamp beyond the far bank seemed to converge with all in a perfect exercise of perspective.

They crossed the turf on the bank and walked down along the trench to where the fire was lit. The fire was in the bottom of the trench because it would be a hazard if lit in any other place. Michael enjoyed dinner-time on the bog; the men sat around while the billy-cans boiled, and spun yarns. They were all from different parts of the country and each man's yarn was usually based in his own homeland with each man moved by an obligation to top the other man's story. The men from the south were by far the best story-tellers and the only one who could compete was Jim O'Donnel from Donegal. Michael seldom spoke, for as soon as he opened his mouth he became conscious of his youth in the company of adults, and he stuttered and forgot what he was about to say. But he was satisfied to listen.

That day the talk moved from the 'back home' yarns to a discussion on gangers. It was dangerous to get on the wrong side of them, everyone agreed. They were ordinary workers like everyone else until they were given the book and pencil; then they walked on all and sundry to show how much they had come on in the world.

'I'll never forget the way they "did in" the German,' said

Christy O'Brien. 'They didn't like him from the start. They used to call him "the Nazi". When the winter came they gave him a German shovel (they said he ought to be able to use it) and put him digging a drain down in the new bog they were reclaiming to open trench seven. They put him on piece-rate. The poor man! No sooner would he have a few yards dug, than the fresh bog would start closing-in again. The gangers would make a point not to call on him to measure the drain until there was no more evidence of a drain than a thin scrape on the surface of the bog. Then they would tell him they couldn't count any drain that wasn't eighteen inches wide at the bottom and that he would have to go back over the whole thing. He had no more than two pounds in wages after the rent for his house was deducted. And there was nothing he could do. He had a wife and family and if he gave up the job they would be thrown out of the house. Well, the German stuck it through the winter, but in February there was a spell of fierce weather to the world; there was sleet and frost; he folded up then; he caught pneumonia; you see his system was run-down for lack of nourishment, and he died.'

That story horrified Michael. He knew the German well, a refugee and a very quiet individual. After his death his wife and family left the district and it was rumoured that they had returned to Germany.

A silence fell over the men when Christy had finished his tale. Each man had a story like it but had no desire to talk; instead they each sat brooding. Michael felt uneasy and turned to Jim O'Donnell.

'What is it like, footing?' he asked.

'It's different,' replied Jim. 'You'll earn more money because you'll be on piece-rate, but you'll work for it.'

There was an ominous ring to the words. At that moment Jim didn't seem anxious to discuss it further and gazed down the bog where the great bagger, humbled by distance, was scooping peat from the bank with monotonous regularity and pumping it out through the long spread-arm for a hundred yards; every two minutes there was a flash as the plates of the spreadarm dipped to drop the new line of sods on the bank.

'What are the plots like at the top of the bank?' Christy

asked generally.

'They're fairly good,' replied a youngish labourer that Michael didn't know. 'I passed them the other day and they seemed to be fairly good.'

'I think we ought to go up this evening and take a plot each; tomorrow the whole bog will be flooded with men, women, and children.'

They all nodded their heads to Christy's suggestion. It was agreed. That evening as the half-past-five locomotive chugged up the rails towards the yard, the men jumped one after another from the wagon doorway. They climbed over the clamp of turf and came to the beginning of the bank. The turf was dry and light and each man took a plot, marking it by footing a row of turf along the top. Michael took a plot. This type of footing was new to him as he was used to the traditional method of standing the sods on their ends and propping them against one another, a method always employed with hand-won turf. Now he had to lay two sods on the ground with a little space between them and across them he had to lay two more; thus he continued building until the footing was about two feet high.

When the men had finished their rows they departed and Michael was left alone on the bog. At first the peace and solitude pleased him; however, after a little while he grew lonely; and soon after that the intensity of the silence began to terrify him, for there wasn't a sign of movement in the whole expanse of bog, and not so much as a bird's whistle to suggest the existence of a single living thing. Michael finished his row as quickly as he could and before leaving made a note of the number that was written on a timber lath at the top of the plot.

The next morning there were hundreds of people on the turf bank. There were men and women, boys and girls. The sight of so many people suggested an atmosphere of festivity and Michael rejoiced in the prospect of companionship. The dark brown of the up-turned sods in the footings contrasted with the light brown of the spread-turf; and the dark brown ran in an ever-widening line along the top of the turf-bank.

Michael found it easy to get into the rhythm of footing in the new manner, but being stooped all the time, his back soon began to stiffen. When he straightened up it ached terribly. He made slow but steady progress and was not far behind the rest at dinner-time.

As usual, at one o'clock he gathered up his coat and bag and set off in the direction of the fire. However, there were very few of the men stopping. Jim O'Donnell had his young son in the bog and was sending him to make the tea, while Christy O'Brien and three other men had joined together so that one could fetch the tea while the others continued working. At the fire there were only a few children waiting for cans and kettles to boil and Michael had to eat his dinner alone.

When he was returning to his plot people were sitting down for their meal; but no sooner had he started to work again than they resumed working also. He was well behind everyone now, but he wasn't worried as his father was coming in the evening to help him.

Michael was very tired by six o'clock and was relieved and happy to see the familiar gait of his father coming up along the trench. His father had a billy-can full of hot tea and they both sat down and ate.

When they had finished eating they set to work once more.

'I was looking at the plots as I was coming up the bog,' said his father, 'and there are some very bad ones down in the hollow. They should be taken up by the time you have this one finished though. If they aren't, try and avoid having to take one. You'd be stuck for a week in one of those plots.'

'Are they near them yet?' enquired Michael.

'Ay, they're within a few plots of the real bad ones.'

'I should miss them so. I'm behind everyone, so they will all be up there before me.'

They worked for an hour and a half, and made rapid progress. Then his father, finishing a row, said: 'I think we'll quit. You have done enough for today. It's heavy work and there's no use killing yourself.'

As they left the bog Michael noticed that few people had ceased working yet.

After two days the plot was almost finished and early on the third day Michael was ready for his second plot. He walked down the bank which was now covered with dark brown

footings for a distance of half-a-mile. Most people were finished their plots, and many seemed to be taking a rest, lying
at the base of the clamp.

When Michael reached the end of the footings he threw
down his bag and coat and took the next vacant plot. It was
down in a hollow and the turf was wet and soft where water
had lodged. In addition, the rows were pitched very closely
together so that each sod was stuck to the next and they
were difficult to separate. When he put them on a footing
they frequently crumbled.

Before he was half-way through his first row many people
arrived: the next plot was quickly taken and the next and the
next. Michael was surprised to see Christy O'Brien and others
now taking plots: he thought that Christy had finished his
one the evening before. A suspicion led him on a walk past
the new plots and he saw that the turf in them was dry and
well spaced. He returned to his own: it was soggy and ugly-
looking. He had been cheated.

Michael felt like crying. He cursed bitterly under his breath
at the people in the succeeding plots; he'd show them. He
tackled the turf again with determination and speed. But the
sods disintegrated in his hands; they were wet and heavy, and
by the time he put the fourth pair on a footing the whole
structure collapsed.

That evening his father moaned when he saw the plot.

'Didn't I tell you to watch out, that they were bad down
here in the hollow. Sure you won't have this done before
Christmas. How in the name of Christ did you get this and
all the people that were finished before you.'

'I think they were holding back and waiting for this one
to be taken. They all came as soon as I had started.'

'Of course they did,' said his father, 'and they're all
laughing at you now, the bastards.'

Michael looked into the gulf of disappointment in his
father's eyes and he was frightened. He looked away, at the
bent figures strung out along the bog; he had hatred in his
heart.

His father started to work without a further word; that
evening they did a quarter of the amount they had done on
the previous evenings. The next day Michael brought his

young brother, Tommy, to the bog; Tommy made the tea in the morning and at dinner-time — Michael no longer wanted to go to the fire for his dinner — and did some footing as well.

Towards evening they were visited by the ganger. He came slowly down through the rows of footings, examining them, poking them with a white lath he had in his hand.

'Good God, Young Conway,' he bellowed, 'this isn't bloody well good enough.' He kicked over a little pile of mud which Tommy had managed to stick together from the debris of sods that had fallen apart in his hands.

'They're awful wet,' Michael looked up, fixing his eyes on the white collar and the brown tie, not daring to look into the fat red face, into the malevolent eyes.

'Well if you're not able to foot them, there's a simple solution: you can get out on the road, and don't let me see your arse for the dust rising after you.'

Michael felt sick and lonely. He thought of the money he had to earn; he remembered his father's expectations of him; he couldn't get the sack. The trousers of the ganger's grey suit were tucked neatly into a shiny new pair of wellingtons. On the toe of his right wellington was a round wet mark where he had kicked over Tommy's footing.

'Sorry, Mr. Griffin, I'll try to do them better,' said Michael meekly.

'You'll bloody well have to do them better,' growled the ganger. 'And what's more you'll have to go back over every bloody footing that you've done. I want to see them all twice as high as they are.'

The ganger stalked off. Michael looked at the footings; they had taken four times as long as usual and now they had to be re-done. He went back to two of the footings and tried to build one on top of the other. They just crumbled underneath the extra weight. He would have to wait and ask his father what to do. Yet he dreaded having to tell him for he still sensed his disappointment of the evening before.

He turned to Tommy who was looking helplessly at his little row of mounds.

'Can't you do them a bit better?' said Michael crossly. 'We'll never get this plot done.'

'But they won't stay together. They break,' explained Tommy.

'Well if you can't do them, go and make the tea. If you're no use on the bog you'll have to stay at home.'

When his father came in the evening, Michael told him all that the ganger had said. He hoped that he would be angry and curse the ganger and the other people and even him: but no, his father was silent and the only reaction he showed was one of hurt. Michael asked him what they should do, but he didn't reply. Without taking his tea, he started to work on the top of the plot, taking the footings apart, enlarging the base and building them higher. Michael followed suit. Tommy was about to join them when his father motioned him to sit down where he was.

They spent that evening going over the previous evening's work. All the while his father never spoke to Michael, and at the usual time they gathered up their coats and bags and went home.

Two days later all the plots in their vicinity were finished and the people had moved on. Michael and Tommy were alone and they were still only half-way through the plot. However, Michael was relieved in so far as the ganger would have to move with the new work and would have little opportunity of coming back to check on them. Sure enough they didn't see a ganger for the next three days and by that time they had the plot done. It had taken them just over a week.

It was late in the afternoon when Michael and Tommy again walked down the trench; it took them half-an-hour to reach the place where the people were now working. When they arrived at the first vacant plot Michael examined it thoroughly. He was determined not to be caught out again. It was poor, though not as bad as the one he had just finished. He examined the plot after that and saw that it was very good.

'Come on,' said he to Tommy and he climbed over the turf clamp. When he got to the other side he unpacked the bag and sent Tommy to make the evening tea.

Every five minutes Michael peeped over the clamp to see if the plot was taken. After some time he saw a man coming down along the top of the bank. Michael hid again and hoped that the man would take the bad plot. He listened intently; presently he heard the rumble of dry turf as the man came clambering over the clamp. A knowing half-smile, an embarrassed nod, were exchanged. The man opened his bag and began to gnaw at a sandwich.

Michael felt uneasy about peeping over the clamp in the presence of the man. He glanced over at him but there was no sign of him to keep a look-out. At length his impatience overcame him: he stood up pretending to stretch himself. The plot was not yet taken. He looked up the bog. A woman and two children were coming down along the bank. Michael's pulse beat faster with anticipation. He knew the woman. She was a Mrs. Murphy and she worked on the bog every summer since her husband deserted her. Would she take it?

Crouching down behind the clamp, Michael was breathless with suspense. He listened and waited, and listened. Eventually his curiosity got the better of him. He peeped over at the plot. She had taken it! Michael hopped across the clamp and hurried to grab the next plot.

The Alchemist of Ballykillcash

The square stone tower, the home of the Alchemist, crowned the hill of Ballykillcash. Its brooding presence dominated the whole countryside from the foothills of the Ox Mountains to the shingle beaches of Templeboy and from the mouth of the Owenmore to the flowing estuary of the Moy. But, to the variations of the rolling landscape the tower presented a solid blind wall; its great windows gazed, instead, northwards over an endless expanse of ocean.

From the shadowy recesses of the tower, the Alchemist was wont to sit looking through these windows; in the winter he watched the angry edge of the wave gashing the cliff-head at Aughris; in the summer he saw the seals splashing silver water and the curlew wading languidly through the ebbed tide.

Years of meditating the boundless ocean, years of experiment and study and observation had bestowed a wisdom above the ordinary on the Alchemist. The local farmers, who never heard nor cared to hear of the elixir or the philosopher's stone, drove their sick beasts to the door of the tower in the hope and expectation of a curative potion. Seldom were they disappointed, and never were they turned away without a pat of sympathy or a word of encouragement. Indeed if these country people were pressed to say what was the most valuable service the Alchemist had done them, they would have to admit it was the indomitable optimism which he continually dispensed. For, in spite of the labyrinthine paths he had wandered in search of truth, in spite of the complex and cryptic symbols that crowded his ancient volumes, the Alchemist had arrived at a simple creed which his unschooled neighbours even could grasp to a small degree: all things are

40

made of prime matter and all change is merely a shift in the accidental properties of things; if all things are capable of change then all things are capable of improvement. And often when they were compelled by circumstances into a dignified acceptance of defeat, shaking their heads, and reconciling themselves with such a traditional assurance as, 'you can't make a silk purse out of a sow's ear,' they would be surprised by the brisk little question from the Alchemist: 'Why not?'

His unlearned neighbours, therefore, had a deep-rooted love and respect for the Alchemist and his quaint ways. They provided for him as they provided for their own families from the abundance of their harvest; even when the wind blew cold and the crops were stunted and sodden, they shared their meagre rations with the eccentric scholar in the tower. They dismissed, without serious consideration, the rumour that he could make golden nuggets with the intricate apparatus to be glimpsed in his laboratory; instead, they believed that the Alchemist was engaged in some learned pursuit which had no relevance to them and which they could never hope to understand.

Yet there was one man in Tireragh who had total faith in the Alchemist's ability to create gold out of the dross beneath his feet, and he was the King, Feardorcha. For a long time now the King had endured with anger and indignation the Alchemist's refusal to fill his coffers with glittering sovereigns. And lately he had sent a horseman to Ballykillcash with an ultimatum: unless the Alchemist provided the gold which King Feardorcha needed for an impending war against the neighbouring King of Tirawley, then all the privileges and property with which the Alchemist had been endowed would be withdrawn and the old scholar would be driven from the kingdom in the same condition as he had once entered it — alone and penniless.

The Alchemist had decided not to respond to this challenge immediately and waited three days before setting out for the King's castle at Easkey.

When he was admitted to the cobble-stoned courtyard the Alchemist detected a putrid odour emanating from the river which flowed within the battlements of Feardorcha's castle. Going over to the pier he inspected the water which poured through the stone arches of the fortress and noticed a number of salmon and trout floating silver-bellied and lifeless along the surface of the stream.

A guard ushered him into the hall. Within moments the King entered, agitated and aggressive, and paced around the floor while he spoke to the Alchemist.

'You have failed me, Fionntan,' he hissed in a tone septic with resentment. 'If you come not with gold, I would rather see you come dead. I gave you everything you asked. I built your tower to your own specifications. I furnished it. I procured your books from distant quarters. And I left you undisturbed for years to perfect your art. Now when it is my turn to need, when I ask you to help me, you refuse. Is this gratitude? Is this fair dealing? But enough, no more! If you will not give me gold I will go elsewhere. Already I have found a man, and he is at work. Soon I will have all the gold I need. And you, Fionntan, you will be walking the roads like a beggar.'

'It grieves me to hear one who was a great and wise King speak thus,' replied the Alchemist. 'I have always told you that my gold was not of the vulgar kind. I am not a manufacturer of sovereigns. Philosophy is my pursuit, and the perfection of nature. Give me a man with a soul of lead and I will exercise my art to transmute that lead to purest gold. Give me a mind where the darkness of Pluto abounds and I will seek to impregnate it with rays of the divine sun.'

'Sovereigns are what I want and not philosophy,' interrupted Feardorcha. 'I can't equip an army on philosophy. But never mind. I have found an alchemist who has promised me sovereigns.'

'I have heard of your alchemist, Leopold the Puffer, and of his ludicrous pretensions. Indeed I have seen the tower which your workmen are erecting for him, on the model of my own, at Rathlee. I watched and I was amused, as you should be, Feardorcha. Anything which is constructed of haste and rubble is destined to fall, and your hopes in him are likewise doomed to disappointment. Leopold will never achieve the first stage of the Great Process, let alone the final stage. To stimulate metals towards their own purification, one must first have effected this metamorphosis within oneself; but

Leopold is the basest man I know. His only motivation is
greed, and he must therefore debase anything he touches,
just as he is now debasing the name of Alchemy.'

'I have listened too long to your sermonising, Fionntan.
Leopold has promised me gold. What have you ever promised me?'

'You never asked anything of me, until you lately demanded coins, vile coins to help you deal slaughter and destruction
to the people of Tirawley, aye and to the people of Tiereragh
too. Had you come in innocence to seek your dearest wishes
I would have striven, even to the utmost of my powers, to
see that they were fulfilled.'

The King chuckled a cold and mirthless laugh. He made an
exaggerated courtesy to the Alchemist. 'Excuse me,' he
mocked, 'here I come in innocence seeking my dearest wishes.
'Please, sir, I would sincerely love to have my dearest wishes.'

'Then you shall have them,' declared the Alchemist maintaining a tone of haughty detachment. 'Think carefully, Feardorcha, and state three wishes. Choose carefully, lest you
should live to rue your own wishes.'

But the King continued to mock. 'I would not offend you,
Fionntan, by wishing for gold or for victory in battle. But I
would not object to three modest little wishes being granted
me. So my first wish is that my son should be the greatest
and most powerful King that Tiereragh has ever known. My
second wish is to extort from my enemy, the King of Tirawley, his most precious possession. My third wish, oh yes,
my third wish is that the bountiful River Easkey which
always carried salmon to my kitchen door be cleansed of
whatever curse has lately befallen her and once again abound
in fish.'

'So be it,' declared the Alchemist. 'Tomorrow morning see
that your son reports to my tower. His training will be long
and rigorous but he shall be the greatest King that Tiereragh
has ever known. Your other wishes likewise shall be granted.'

With that he turned and left the castle.

* * *

For nine months Conall, son of Feardorcha, lodged with the Alchemist who took the unwrought soul of this young prince and manipulated it, stage by stage, through the seven phases of the Great Process

One: *dissolution into a state of flux.*
Two: *purification through the precipitation of dross.*
Three: *firing in a heated furnace.*
Four: *death and putrefaction leading to ressurection.*
Five: *multiplication.*
Six: *fermentation, a slow process during which the multiple becomes integrated.*
Seven: *projection.*

And when he had finished, the Alchemist was satisfied with his work.

* * *

The monks of Rosserk Abbey in the kingdom of Tirawley were close friends of the Alchemist. So, when he sent a messenger to them to find out what was their ruler's most treasured possession, they replied that, unquestionably, his most treasured possession was his only daughter, Caitriona. Moreover, they agreed to arrange an interview between the Princess and the Alchemist.

On a dark and dreary evening in January the Alchemist and Conall circled the shore of Killala Bay and arrived at Rosserk as the torches were being lit in the cloisters. They were received by the Abbot and taken to the refectory where food was laid out on a table for them. A lively fire burned in the hearth. But a warmer glow was cast around the room from the presence of a young girl sitting quietly near the fire. The Abbot introduced her as Caitriona, the daughter of Fergus, King of Tirawley. The wily Alchemist observed the glances which were exchanged between Conall and Caitriona and he knew immediately that his mission was going to be successful.

They spent the evening in conversation, sometimes witty, sometimes sad; they laughed at stories of trivial follies; they listened to the harp-music of a bard who was lodging for a short time at the abbey. And all the while the attraction between Caitriona and Conall became stronger and waxed into friendship, and the friendship grew into love. By the time the bell tolled the hour of sleep they had shared an evening of unlimited delight; though no words were spoken nor vows exchanged, a bond of mutual sympathy was forged between them stronger than steel and far more lasting

Early the following morning, as they prepared to leave the abbey the Alchemist invited Caitriona to visit with him at Ballykillcash, and told her to convey to her father his personal guarantee of her safety. Conall bade a graceful farewell to the girl, and, as he did so, she pressed a small embroidered napkin into his hand, saying: 'You must keep this carefully for me until I come to collect it.'

Trudging homewards through the snow Conall held the token as if it were a precious thing. He skipped along ahead of the amused Alchemist. Passing through the Woods of Kilglass his high spirits overflowed: he cast his spear into the boughs of an oak tree where a raven sat brooding. The spear scored a direct hit and the raven fell dead in the path of the young prince, its breast pierced by the point of the lance.

Conall was shocked by the sight of the dead raven, its blood beginning to trickle on to the snow. He knelt down before it and began to weep.

'Behold my love in torment,' he cried.

'What do you mean?' asked the Alchemist.

'Her hair is as black as the raven's wing; the red blood is the very pigment of her lips; and the snow, the snow is her white body. What agony have I inflicted on my love? The beauty of the whole world lies here, fragile, bleeding, maimed by a wanton act.'

He dipped the napkin in the red blood of the raven, watched the stain soak into the fabric, and then placed the sacred token in a pocket close to his heart.

'Nevermore shall any act of mine cause needless pain.

Nevermore will I defile the innocence of this earth with the barbarous streaks of savage butchery.'

With that he grasped the spear and broke its shaft in two across his knee.

The Alchemist consoled Conall.

'You have learned well,' said he, 'for you have divined the wisdom of the symbolic image. Your education is complete.'

Within a week Caitriona arrived at the Alchemist's tower. She was accompanied by an unarmed escort of two horsemen, but they returned to Tirawley as soon as their princess was delivered safely to her destination. Before she had alighted from her horse, Conall was at her side, reaching to help her down. As their fingers met their love was re-affirmed and guaranteed in the magical sensation of that touch.

After dinner while Conall and Caitriona sat in the Alchemist's upper room gazing out of its great windows, the old man announced: 'tomorrow you must undertake a task. You wish to be united in love, but true unity of mind, and soul, and body, occurs only in joint endeavour, in combined effort, in working together, like oxen yoked to the one plough. At dawn you will set out to trace the course of the Easkey River, which has been unwholesome to fish for more than a year now, and try to discover what is contaminating it.'

At first light the following morning Conall and Caitriona proceeded to the ford at Ballinahoilte. Conall sampled the water and found it contaminated so he knew that the source of contamination was further up. He took one bank of the river and Caitriona took the other. They made their way slowly up through the wooded valley, testing each tributary stream as they went along. By evening they had reached the foothills of the Ox Mountains and had not yet discovered what was polluting the river. They rested for a while and ate the food they had brought. Then they started the slow ascent of the mountainside where the thin river fell fitfully among the rocks and bracken. The light was fading rapidly over the sea when Caitriona called out:

'Conall, look.'

She had discovered a shallow mine or pit dug into the mountainside. The earth was fresh, so the mine was still being worked. Out of the mouth of the shaft a drain led down to the river, and a continuous flow of greenish-yellow sludge dribbled into the clear waters. Conall dipped his hand into the sludge and smelt the same repulsive odour which had been rising off the river all the way down to his father's castle.

'Who do you think is responsible for this?' asked Caitriona.

'The only person in this kingdom who would be mining sulphur is Leopold, an abominable creature who masquerades as an alchemist and whom my father has employed to make gold. It is ironic how the fates punish us with our own deeds. My father's greed has caused the poisoning of this river, this same river which was his very pride and joy.'

'Come, let us try to block-off the drain, and prevent any more of that filth entering the river, at least until workmen can come and close the pit,' suggested Caitriona.

They rolled in a few small boulders to form a dam and packed it with stones and sand. Caitriona strove and strained at this labour until her hands were chapped and her dress was smudged and ripped. Satisfied that they had stopped the flow of the virulent sludge, they rested for a short while. It was now dark and the clear frosty sky displayed its full array of winking stars. To Conall and Caitriona the stars seemed to be pulsating with their joy, sharing the ecstasy of their union, a union cemented by the labours of that day as the Alchemist had guaranteed. When they thought of the old scholar they looked towards the tower in the distance. The moon hung like a great silver disk overhead and silhouetted the stone structure against the line of the sea.

When they had retraced the long journey back to the tower the Alchemist was waiting for them, anxious to hear about their discovery; but when they told him of the sulphur pit he did not appear surprised; in fact it merely confirmed a theory which he had held since he had first sniffed the pungent smell of the water at Easkey.

'I think it would be proper to go now and present ourselves to the King,' said he.

'But we are exhausted from our journey and our labour,' replied Caitriona. 'Our clothes are torn to rags and we are covered in filth. We are in no fit condition to greet a King.'

'My dear girl,' the Alchemist smiled as he spoke, 'exhaustion is relative to the importance of the task in hand. And as for your appearance, even if you were adorned with all the silk and jewels of the east, you could not appear more noble than you do now, smeared as you are with the dirt of toil.'

King Feardorcha was indeed perplexed when he was roused out of his early morning sleep. Peering from his balcony into the half-light of the courtyard he barely discerned the person of the Alchemist but was at a complete loss as to the identity of the two squalid figures accompanying him. He pulled his robe about him and descended the stone steps. The Alchemist bowed and addressed him.

'I may be no better than a beggar, Feardorcha, but I have come to grant a King his wishes: irony, as you may have perceived, is the very guiding principle of the universe. Your wish was that the Easkey River should be cleansed of its curse. I must inform you that the curse was of your own making. The river was poisoned by the voracious Leopold clawing ignorantly at the sides of the mountain. The emission from his sulphur pit, which was contaminating the river, has been blocked, but you had better send a squad of workmen to close the pit thoroughly.'

Feardorcha was taken aback by this revelation. He replied: 'If Leopold is responsible for the pollution of this river, as you allege, Fionntan, he shall not breathe the air of this kingdom for another day.'

'Your wish was to extort from the King of Tirawley his most precious possession,' continued the Alchemist. 'Before you is Caitriona the daughter of Fergus, King of Tirawley, acknowledged by one and all to be his dearest possession. She is betrothed to your son. Therefore you have your wish, whether it pleases you or not.'

'Maybe so, but what of my son. You promised to make him into a great King. He was a comely prince when you took him into your charge. Look at him now. My meanest servant is better clad and better presented.'

'Your son and his princess wear the emblems of labour; they have come directly from restoring the health of your river. Thanks to them, when the new season comes, the stream will be once more heavy with fish. You do not appear to have acquired insight or wisdom since our last meeting. But your son, on the other hand, has acquired both. He now has the wisdom and the strength of character to rule this kingdom. But your wish that he should become a great King, is forestalled by your own incumbency: while you continue to occupy the throne Conall cannot be a King. It would be unlucky and unworthy of you, Feardorcha, to let your lust for power prevent the fulfilment of your own expressed wish for your son. My advice is, therefore, that you set a date for your abdication. Think on it, Feardorcha. Perhaps the world is still too young, too innocent, to be entrusted to the care of crusty old men.'

The King listened to the Alchemist and could not refute his reasoning. Powerless as a lone chess-piece on a board, he had to concede defeat. Nor could he find it in his mind to cavil at the ironic justice of the outcome. Graciousness was his last option. He studied Conall, the set lines in his face, the new determined piercing look in his eye, the calm self-possession evident on his brow. He examined Caitriona, the beauty of her features, the tender warmth of her nature, the endearing smudge of toil in which she was unashamedly covered.

'Your logic is relentless, Fionntan, and of course you are right. This world is no fit place for crusty old men, preoccupied with war and wealth and power. I will rule my kingdom until Samhain. But when the fires of the New Year are blazing, let them burn for the nuptials of this young couple and for the investiture of a new King.'

Depths

I almost strained my eyes peering through the small round windows of the aeroplane. The object — my first glimpse of New York. The plane banked and circled on its approach to Kennedy Airport and my wish was granted — a total view of the city laid out before me. Not the distant prospect of the Statue of Liberty through the railings of an ocean-weary ship! I could see every street, every house, every motor-car, every human being, all miniatured into the one picture; all comprehended in the one exhaustive gaze. As the plane dived and skimmed over the streets, the houses became bigger, the diminutive cars began to look like viable toys, the people who were dots grew so big even their faces were visible, and then I closed my eyes, afraid lest they should reciprocate my staring.

My cousin was waiting for me at the terminal. I tried to be calm and casual, knowing that I was expected to be the opposite because I was sixteen and from Ireland. He had his wife with him, his children, and the children's nanny. I felt secure in the warmth of their welcome.

How they found their car among the million in the parking lot, I thought, was a small miracle. They drove a special route home in order to show me the best profile of the Manhatten skyline, pointing at intervals to the rising pinacles in front of us as we sped along the Long Island Expressway.

The glass towers rose up into the evening sky, touching the red sun and scattering its light. And I knew I was in New York. There was excitement in my veins, excitement in the babble of the children at the back of the car, excitement in the six lanes of traffic careering towards the glass towers and the setting sun.

* * *

BUT A SCREAM WAS BORN DEEP IN THE EARTH AND IT GREW AND GREW UNTIL IT BURST AND FILLED THE CITY, HOOKING ITS DESPERATE FINGERS AROUND THE GLASS TOWERS AND SQUEEZING UNTIL THEY WERE SHATTERED AND STIFLED.

* * *

The coughing had ceased but he continued holding his head over the edge of the bed, staring at the blobs on the floor. He rubbed his finger in the dark-red liquid and examined it more closely. It was blood. The shock, the terror, gripped violently at his bowels. Had he vomited it, or had it come up with the coughing? Hastily he re-experienced the spasm, but could not recall his stomach heaving. It must have come up with the coughing. He knew what that meant. He was going to die. Clutching the pillow he stuffed it in his mouth for fear he would roar. There was no one to summon, no one to help him. Less that a year in America, he still felt thousands of miles from home. There were the two friends of his father who had brought him out and set him up with a job in the foundry, but his tenuous relationship with them had not thrived in the new environment. What could he do? Where could he go? He thought of his mother and the way she used to nurse him when he had a cold. And he wept. Great sobs were muffled in the pillow. He tried to control himself, fearing he would preciptate another bout of coughing. Getting out of the bed he walked the narrow space surrounding it within the shabby room. The silence terrified him. He listened intently. Faint sounds of distant motor-cars only intensified the silence of the room. He dressed himself and hurried out into the street where, at least, there were people. On the lowest step before the front door he sat down. It was much better outside. The sight of all the pedestrians passing within arm's length of him soothed his loneliness and he remembered that he had sixty dollars saved, enough to pay his fare back to Ireland.

* * *

Since childhood I had nurtured images of Coney Island. Through long brooding it had come to represent the final distillation of pleasure: commonplace America was to me the land of youth and happiness, but Coney Island was where the Americans went to enjoy themselves.

With composed curiosity I surveyed the expanse of amusement parks. All possible attractions were there, chair-planes, round-abouts, bumping-cars, roller coasters. But what most fascinated me was the boarded sidewalks. Clip-clip-clip-clip went my footsteps and I teased my brain trying to remember some gangster film I had seen. I walked up and down, scarcely attending to the gambling halls and the ice cream parlours, listening to the sound of my own footsteps. Perhaps because it reminded me of something old, I detected a melancholy atmosphere over that shrine of pleasure.

My cousin's little daughter appeared in her swimsuit and catching my hand, tugged me down to the water's edge. There were thousands of children running about in the shallow water, laughing and playing, splashing and shouting.

* * *

BUT THE SCREAM DARKENED THE SKY, CHILLING THE BODIES OF THE CHILDREN AND SILENCING THEIR JOY.

* * *

Too weak to get out of bed now, he lay with his head tilted towards the door. He was listening for the landlady's footsteps on the stairs. But she seldom came and, when she did, she grumbled about the blood-stains on the bed-clothes and the two weeks' arrears of rent. In spite of that he longed to hear her approach, because if a letter came from home it was she who would bring it to him. It had taken him two months to decide whether to return to Ireland or not. Two

*weeks ago he had made his decision. If he had gone home he
would have burdened his family with the anguish of death,
with the example of his failure, and with the expense of his
funeral. They had scrimped and borrowed for his fare over
and had staked their future on his success. How could he let
them down? So a fortnight ago he had taken his last forty
dollars to the Telegraph Office and sent it to his mother
with a note to say he was prospering in the new country.*

*Already he was expecting a reply. All the previous letters
he had received from home were tucked under his pillow, and
he took them out several times a day to re-read them. Since
he had sent off the last of his money he had had no food to
eat. But that would shorten his suffering. Although he
was resigned to death he was afraid he would die before the
letter came. He wanted to know that the money had arrived;
he wanted to read how delighted and grateful they were; he
wanted to hear the things they were planning to do with the
money.*

*It was a summer's night and the darkness was heavy with
warmth. Half-past ten! Twilight would be still lingering over
Tireragh. What cool breezes would be blowing in from the sea
over the stony beaches! He would die a thousand deaths if
he could just live one more evening in Tireragh, or if he could
be buried in her congenial soil.*

* * *

My holiday was nearly over now, but there was one obligation I had to fulfil before I left. I had to visit my Uncle
William's grave. The eldest of my father's family, he had gone
to America in 1930 where he died within a few months. My
father had reminded me to visit the grave, but had forgotten
to tell me where it was. Perhaps he didn't know! Perhaps he
thought it would be common knowledge in New York!

However, my cousin contacted someone and found out exactly where William was buried. On the day before I was to
leave we made our pilgrimage to Calvary Cemetery. My cousin
led the way according to directions and I followed, carrying a bunch of flowers, full of wonder that after forty years
I would be the first of William's family to visit his grave.

Eventually my cousin stopped and pointed: 'This is the place. How nice! They've turned it into a park.' I looked. There were no gravestones and the ground was levelled. Women and old men sat on benches watching, while black children were playing noisily on the grass. I stood there staring at the ground under the children's feet, wishing they would tread more gently, wondering why the earth was not groaning beneath them. A little girl with jet-black skin and hair in tiny plaits came near me. I called her and gave her the bunch of flowers. She ran off to show them to her mammy.

* * *

THE SCREAM GREW IN MY HEART, EXPLODING IN MY MIND, LIKE THE DYING BREATH OF A MILLION NAMELESS MEN GROANING THEIR DESPERATION TO THE SKIES.

The Thane of Cawdor Lives

1

Charles Betson, Secretary of the Department of Social Development, arrived in his office at eight thirty on the morning of 13 October. The building was still lifeless at that hour; the long arteries of corridors had not yet begun to circulate their daytime vitality. He had to while away a full hour pacing about his carpeted floor, sitting moments at a time in his plush armchair, gazing out the window at the treetops in the park outside.

Eventually, Scanlon, his personal messenger, came through the door in his mechanical way and left the morning's first deposits in the green 'IN' tray. He exited, as he had entered, without acknowledging the Secretary, or registering the least surprise in seeing the boss behind his desk at this unprecedented hour. The Secretary rummaged through the tray. He disregarded the unopened letters marked 'Personal' and the files with glaring red tage which read 'For your urgent attention.' In the bottom of the tray he found the three morning papers. Taking these out he returned to his desk.

He spread out the papers in front of him. The headlines of each predicted a landslide victory for the Left-Wing Coalition in that day's general election. Was there no hope at all?

Skimming through the columns he saw a reference to his own Department. It said that if the Coalition were to win the election the Socialist Party would be given the Ministry of Social Development; the Socialists, it said, had been critical of the policy of this Department for many years and were determined to bring about a fundamental change.

Yes, he had heard that rumour before now. He had also heard that the Socialists would get rid of him from his post of Secretary. Uneasy as he was, the Secretary was scornful of that threat; he was butressed by the traditional belief that it was as difficult to sack a civil servant as to pass an Act of Parliament.

He folded the papers and laid them on the side-table. At that moment he would have been glad of someone to talk to, someone to reassure him that the outcome of the election might not be so disastrous. But there was nobody. He had three Assistant Secretaries, but these he kept in a permanent state of submission and humiliation; it was the safest way to have them, the only way he could feel secure; for if any of them were to entertain ambitions it could only bode danger for him. He did not intend to leave himself open on that front. Had not a simple telephone-call to the press toppled his predecessor?

Under the Assistant Secretaries there were fifteen Principal Officers. These he treated with the contempt normally reserved for office boys. The other grades, containing hundreds of men and women, were all the same to the Secretary, an amorphous body which he continually pounded and stamped to ensure its subjection. He could walk up and down the corridor a hundred times, but he would not meet a single person who would dare to look him in the face. He could walk into any office and there wasn't a man who could sit easily on his chair. The Secretary liked it that way, for he didn't trust a single individual in the whole department.

Scanlon was about the only one he trusted, not so much trusted as felt free to disregard. Well, there was nothing Scanlon could gain from injury to him. He would not be looking for promotion. The man was scarcely literate: when he was decyphering the title of a file his lips moved involuntarily, shaping each syllable in slow succession. He performed his duties with such regularity and disinterest that he might be a robot.

The Secretary rang the bell to summon his trusty robot.

'Fetch me the file on George Duffy. You'll get it from the Personnel Section.'

Scanlon went off obediently. Duffy was a thorn in the

Secretary's side. Although he was only a Junior Executive Officer of three years' standing he was brazenly indiscreet about his affiliation to the Socialist Party. Reports had conveyed to the Secretary that Duffy had addressed the Annual Conference of that Party and had criticised the Department of Social Development for alleged lack of initiative. After that incident the Secretary had warned him in plain terms to stay away from politics, but the warning had fallen on deaf ears. Duffy had been seen canvassing support for the Socialists all through the current election campaign.

Scanlon returned with the file and placed it on his desk. The Secretary opened it and, as he suspected, he saw that Duffy had taken a day's leave on that day. It was so blatant! But he wouldn't escape this time; he would be nailed finally. The Secretary knew the area in which Duffy had been canvassing, and surmised that he would be spending the day outside the polling booth for that area.

He wrote a note for the Personnel Officer: *'I suspect that Mr Duffy has taken a day's leave today to canvass support for a political party. I expect that he will be in the vicinity of the polling booth at Inchicore. Drive over there on you way back from lunch and check. Report to me on your return.'*

Pinning the note to the file he rang again for Scanlon.

'Take this down to the Personnel Officer,' he ordered.

The Secretary was beginning to feel pleased with himself. Duffy was bound to be there and he would be caught. And when he was caught he would be appropriately punished; he deserved demotion at the very least. It was one point on which the rules were totally explicit, so there could be no appeal, no redress.

But what if the Personnel Officer covered up for him? Suppose that he warned Duffy off, or pretended that he wasn't there; what then? No, he couldn't leave it to the Personnel Officer. He rang the bell.

'Did you take that file down to the Personnel Officer?' he asked Scanlon.

'He wasn't in his office, Sir, so I left it on his table,' Scanlon replied.

'Well, bring it back to me.'

So that was the time these dogs came in — just a step ahead

of himself. They had been found-out this morning, and they
would hear about it.

Scanlon returned with the file. The Secretary took it, tore
out the note, and said:

'Okay, bring the file back to the Personnel Section and
tell them to put it away again.'

2

George Duffy had occupied the most strategic position close
to the gate of the polling booth at Inchicore. This was the
battlefield of the Twentieth Century; it was here that power
was lost and won. But you would never think, to look on it,
that it had such significance; for it was no more than a drab
grey schoolhouse, growing shabbier as the day progressed
because of the accumulation of littered handbills. A fine
battlefield indeed! There were two girls from his party with
him and, between the three of them, they intercepted each
voter, thrusting a handbill and an admonition at each. The
people seemed to be responding warmly to them, more so
than to the representatives of the other parties, giving a wink
or an upraised thumb as they passed. This filled Duffy with
unbounded optimism. They would annihilate the conservatives,
as everyone was predicting.

Just before one o'clock he was surprised to see, pedalling
towards him on his bicycle, Ned Scanlon, the messenger in
the Department. What was he doing in this part of the city,
at this time of the day? Scanlon brought his bicycle to a
halt at the kerb nearby and beckoned with his hand. Duffy
went over.

'You'd better get out of here quick,' said Scanlon. 'The
Secretary will be passing here any minute to try and catch
you, and, if he does, you know what's going to happen.'

'Ah, you're joking, Ned. He's not going to come himself —
in person! By God, he must be feeling the pressure.' And he
began to laugh.

'Come on! Hurry up! I don't want to be seen here with

you,' Scanlon urged impatiently.

'All right! We'll nip down to the Black Lion.' Duffy gave his handbills to one of the girls, explaining why he had to leave and where he could be found.

In the snug of the Black Lion Duffy ordered two pints of stout and two ham sandwiches.

'To tell you the truth, Ned, you're the last person in the world I would have expected to come and warn me against the Secretary. I always assumed you were hand-in-glove with him, with you working so close to him. But I'm glad I was wrong and I'm grateful for what you've done.'

'I know the opinion everyone has of me inside in the Department, but I don't care. I don't go around spewing my mind out to all and sundry. However, I'll tell you this much: there will be no man happier than myself if that bastard is shifted.'

'He'll be shifted all right, Ned, never fear. I'll let you in on a secret. I was talking to Dwyer the other day. He's going to be Minister for our Department if we win the election. I asked him how he was going to get rid of Betson, seeing that he couldn't be sacked and was too young to be retired. Well Dwyer clapped me on the shoulder, and says he, 'We'll export him to the E.E.C. The more men of his calibre we have in Brussels mucking up the machinery, the sooner that institution will collapse.'

Duffy gave a loud belly-laugh and repeated, 'We'll export him to the E.E.C.' Scanlon laughed too, though not so exuberantly. The lines of his face were set into a permanent scowl and the deep smile he gave tightened and distorted his features.

'I was thinking this morning that he doesn't know any French or German. He will have to start swotting,' continued Duffy, laughing. 'Wouldn't it be a nice idea for the presentation, Ned — a Linguaphone French Course. Can you imagine the speech? '— hoping it will bring you many satisfying hours.' It's not bad, Ned, is it?'

'It's not bad,' agreed Scanlon, his face lapsing into its habitual scowl, 'when you think of the end he gave poor old Donoghue.'

'What do you mean by that, Ned? Donoghue was the

Secretary before him, wasn't he?'

'Ay, Donoghue was the Secretary before him, and he'd still be there if it hadn't been for a dirty deed.'

'I don't follow you, Ned,' said Duffy. 'I heard that Donoghue had to resign because of a scandal. He was involved with a prostitute. She was blackmailing him or something.'

'That's right. But Donoghue was a gentleman to the tips of his fingers. The present so-and-so wouldn't be fit to hold his coat. And the Department was a different place then. You'd feel happy going in the door in the morning. But look at it now. Every man that passes through the door has a curse on his tongue but is terrified to utter it. They're all ready to grovel at the sight of the Secretary. And the higher up they go, the worse they become. You wouldn't believe the level that men can be reduced to. They go in to him and tell tales on each other, just to ward off his anger from their own heads. And does it work? Never. He treats them with even greater contempt, so they have to go off and find something more malicious to tell him. It would open your eyes to see how low men can stoop before a tyrant like that.'

'I've seen something of it myself, Ned. But you mentioned a dirty deed. What was that?'

'I'll tell you all right,' said Scanlon. 'But no one knows about this except myself, so you'd better not spread it around, for the present anyhow. Donoghue was involved with a woman. He was a bachelor, you know. Well, she must have found out about his being the Secretary of the Department. She wrote him a letter demanding money and addressed it to 'The Secretary, Department of Social Development.' So, of course, the letter was opened in the Registry just like all the other letters that come in addressed like that. I don't know exactly what happened then. Either the girl put the letter in the wrong tray, or else he was snooping through Donoghue's mail himself; but however it happened, the letter got into Betson's hands. He was Assistant Secretary in those days. That's how I came to know about it. I was taking files from his office into Donoghue's when he called me back. He took the files from me and pretended to rummage through them. But I saw him slipping the letter in between the files; then he gave them back to me. When I got outside I had a look at

the letter and saw what was in it. The next day the newspaper headline had the story of Donoghue being blackmailed
by a prostitute. It was a big scandal at the time, and he had
to resign, the poor man. Then Betson was made Secretary.'

'Well, I never suspected that before, Ned, but it certainly
sounds like the kind of thing he'd do. By God, his days are
numbered now, though.'

'Take care he doesn't have your guts for garters before he
goes,' warned Scanlon. 'He knows of everything you've been
doing in the last few weeks, and he'll be as sore as a bear
when he didn't catch you today.'

Duffy considered the advice while Scanlon was collecting
two more pints through the service hatch. It wasn't that he
was afraid of anything that the Secretary could do. He could
get another job in the morning, possibly a better one — but
he would hate to give Betson any satisfaction at this stage.
Scanlon returned with the pints.

'I know what I'll do, Ned. I'll get a medical cert. for a
week or fortnight. He won't be able to do anything if I'm not
around to answer charges. By the time I come back the new
Government will be installed and Betson will be learning
French in Brussels.'

Duffy raised his glass which was brimming with froth:
"Here's to the E.E.C., Ned, that has given us new scope
for our exports.'

Scanlon raised his pint to his mouth and drained it in three
or four effortless swallows.

'I must be going,' said he. 'Give me a ring in the office
around half-two and I'll let you know if the Secretary is back.
Then you'll be able to get on with your work.'

And, wiping the froth from his lips, he was off.

The Bleeding Stone of Knockaculleen

I got to the field early with the J.C.B. as I wanted to have the job finished by nightfall. John Patrick Murphy had recently returned from England and had bought this field from Jim Dowd. It was very uneven, being overlaid with mounds and boulders and enveloped in an ample growth of whins. Evidently it had been in that condition for many a long day; I had an Ordnance Survey map at home, drawn in 1837, and it showed all the mounds and scrub just as they still were. John Patrick intended to clear the field and make it a profitable investment, so he asked me to level it. I told him my price and the bargain was made.

It was by no means a big job, so I reckoned six hours would see it complete. In one corner there was a circular mound which looked like a small rath. If I had been superstitious I would have been reluctant to disturb the fairies underneath, but I wasn't; I had bulldozed several of them before, without retaliation. There was one small problem, however: in the middle of the little rath there was a boulder which was too big to be moved by the J.C.B., but I had arranged to get some gelignite to blow it apart. The agent, who was to carry out the job, was due around dinner-time.

I started to work on the side nearest the road, digging away the mounds, filling in the ditches and levelling the ground. It was easy work, and very pleasant on a summer's morning. The field was on top of the hill of Knockaculleen, so I had a tremendous view out over the sea past Aughris Head where the island of Innishmurray was squatting in a blue haze — that was a sign of good weather. From beyond the brow of Ballykillcash I could hear the hum of a tractor mowing a meadow. Men passed by on their bicycles, whistling as they pedalled their way towards the bog (they wouldn't get past the village, if I knew some of them).

Around eleven o'clock John Patrick came across the field with a tin-can in one hand and a string shopping-bag in the other. He hailed me and I knocked off the engine.

'I have a drop of tea here, Pat.'

'And it's welcome too,' said I, 'I was just beginning to feel thirsty.'

We sat on the grass leaning our backs against the wall. John Patrick opened the bag, took out two mugs and set them on the ground. Then he unrolled the sandwiches that his wife had neatly packed and handed one to me. He took the lid off the tin-can and poured two mugs of tea.

It was while we were eating that we saw Tim Foley coming through the open gap. He was very old, thin, slightly stooped, and he walked with the aid of an ash plant. Slowly he made his way over the uneven ground and with difficulty he sat down on a stone beside us.

'That's a fine day, Tim', said John Patrick.

' ''Tis indeed,' replied Tim, 'thanks be to God.'

'How arc they all down in Dromore West?'

'They're all well indeed.'

Tim took out his pipe, tapped it a few times on the base of his thumb, searched in his pocket and produced a piece of plug tobacco, which he proceeded to pare with his pen-knife. Having filled his pipe he struck a series of matches until he finally had the pipe glowing. Puffing away, he pushed back his head and looked about.

'I heard that you were working on the field, so I came up to see it before you had it flattened. It was a grand field. I remember playing here when I was a gasur — no bigger than the stone I'm sitting on. You know, it was a great place for rabbits. Every mound and ditch used to be riddled with rabbit burrows. It was great sport to come up here with a ferret and a hound. You'd catch dozens of them — enough to feed a family for a week.'

'They made a nice dinner, sure enough,' agreed John Patrick, 'but thcy were a curse all the same. You couldn't put down a crop or they'd cut it to bits. I think myself that it was a good idea to get rid of them.'

'I don't know about that,' countered Tim. 'Many a big family was reared on rabbits — what they didn't eat they sold — and they would have been in a bad way if the rabbits weren't there. I wouldn't mind so much if they went out and hunted them down for food; but to bring in a disease to destroy them, ah, that was a crime.'

'It was the only way, Tim. They would never have got rid of them otherwise.'

'Ah, no, it was a crime; it was a crime,' mumbled Tim as he sucked and puffed at his pipe.

'Well, rabbits, or no rabbits, we have to get this field levelled,' said John Patrick, getting up and stretching himself. I got up as well, flexing the stiffness out of my limbs.

'Thanks for the tea, and tell the good woman that her sandwiches were delicious.'

'Don't mention it,' replied John Patrick.

As we were moving away Tim raised his pipe in his right hand: 'Tell me. Are you going to level the rath in the far corner?'

'Of course we are,' answered John Patrick. 'It's all good land and I can't afford to waste any.'

'You shouldn't go near the rath,' said Tim seriously. 'It's been there since the beginning of time and it will bring bad luck on the man who interferes with it.'

'Come on now. You're not going to start telling us about the fairies,' joked John Patrick, and turning to me he asked, 'Do you believe in fairies, Pat?'

I laughed. 'Well, I've bulldozed a few raths before and they haven't hit back at me yet, so I'll chance another one.'

Again we were about to depart when Tim halted us. 'What about the stone that's in the middle of the rath?' he asked.

'That's a bit big for the digger,' I replied, 'but I have a man coming around dinner-time to blow it up.'

Old Tim shook with emotion and stood up on his unsteady legs. 'You're not going to blow up that stone!' he whispered in astonishment.

'Why not?' I asked. 'It's in the way, isn't it?'

'That's no ordinary stone,' hissed Tim. 'That's called the Bleeding-Stone.'

'Well, the bleedin' stone is destroying the corner of my

field and it has to go,' said John Patrick punning deliberately.

'Do you know the legend attached to that stone?' asked Tim, becoming more passionate.

'No,' answered John Patrick. 'And what's more I didn't know there was a legend attached to it.'

'There you are,' said Tim in a tone of mingled irony and triumph. 'You're destroying something and you don't know the value of it. That stone and the story behind it are greater than me and you because we last only one lifetime but they have lasted hundreds of lifetimes.'

'What is the story?' said I, going back to lean against the wall.

'We can't be wasting time listening to the ravelling of an old man,' John Patrick declared impatiently.

'There's no hurry, I'll get the job finished before night.'

'There was a lord in this locality one time,' began Tim, 'whose name was Mac Giolla Cais. He was extremely wealthy and had the finest fort in Tireragh, the remains of which you can see to this day beyond in Carrownrush. Mac Giolla Cais had a beautiful daughter called Aoife and it was said of her that she was as dear to the poorest peasant on the estate as she was to her father.

Once, a poor travelling poet, Art O Connor, arrived at the fort seeking the Lord's patronage. Mac Giolla Cais, a generous patron of learning, thought that the young poet had promise and gave him an honoured place among his household.

When Art saw Aoife he immediately feel deeply in love with her and began to compose the most exquisite lyrics in her praise. At the next feast, when he was summoned by the lord to recite some of his verses, Art chanted those he had written for Aoife. She herself was present and was moved by the sensitive passion of the lyrics so that she, in turn, fell in love with Art, but without realising that the poems were addressed to her.

For many months Art continued to write poems expressing his love and every time he recited them Aoife was his most attentive listener. He never betrayed that it was to her that they were dedicated, for he believed that such a beautiful, such a noble maiden would have little regard for the affections of a poor poet.

As for Aoife, she assumed that Art had a mistress somewhere who was the subject of his poems. Her youthful mind brooded on the hopelessness of her love and she lost interest in food and companionship.

MacGiolla Cais grew anxious about his daughter's well-being and summoned the doctors and druids. But none could tell him what her ailment was.

When she was very weak she asked the servants to carry her to the banquet room so that she could hear the poet. On her arrival Art chanted a new poem he had written expressing his sorrow at his mistress's illness. Aoife, not realising that the poem was for her, thought only of Art's mistress who, in her illness, had such wonderful lyrics to comfort her. Her heart broke between love and despair, and she died, falling at the foot of the dais on which the poet was standing.

All the people of Tireragh were heartbroken at the death of Aoife; so beloved was she that thousands gathered at the fort of Mac Giolla Cais to sympathise with him and to attend her burial. The young men went out beyond the fort to a green spot and dug her grave; around the grave they threw a high mound so that mankind should not forget where she was buried. No sooner was her body laid and covered than a mysterious thorn bush sprang from the spot, budded and flowered in an instant.

Art, in the meantime, was grief-stricken by the death of Aoife. He was requested by Mac Giolla Cais to compose an elegy for the funeral, but he was so paralysed by grief that he could not, and he vowed that he would never again write a verse.

When the funeral was over and the people had dispersed, Art went to the place where Aoife was buried. He threw himself prostrate on the grave. His sorrow was so great that he was unable to utter a single syllable, but he determined to stay there until death should release him to follow his beloved.

Three days and three nights he lay there. On the third night a wind blew from the west and the leaves and the boughs of the thorn bush began to flutter and whisper. As the wind grew stronger the whispering became louder until it was audible and articulate. It was the voice of Aoife telling of her hopeless love for the young poet, Art.

The realisation that Aoife had died for love of him swept over Art as the sea in storm sweeps over a curragh. His horror pressed like a murderous ocean on his soul. And yet death denied him its mercy. But Aengus, son of the Good God, who was always sensitive to the anguish of the lover, became aware of Art's plight. In a twinkling he came. Taking pity on Art, Aengus touched him with his hazel rod and turned him into a rock.

That same rock has rested upon the grave of Aoife from that day to this. It is said that if anyone tries to move it from its beloved spot, the rock will bleed. That is why it became known as the Bleeding-Stone.'

Old Tim paused when he had finished the story. His eyes had a distant look; but the distance into which he was looking was not outside him: it was somewhere deep within. He took his pipe from his mouth and examined it; it had quenched for lack of attention while Tim was involved in his story. Striking a match he asked:

'You wouldn't move that stone, would you?'

John Patrick turned angrily to me: 'For Christ's sake, will you get to work and stop wasting time listening to shit like that. If that frigging rock is there for a couple of thousand years it's bloody well time that someone shifted it.'

I got up on the J.C.B. and started digging again. Old Tim was watching me closely. I felt sorry for him in a way; every time the bucket sliced into the earth it seemed as if it was cutting into his own flesh. Old lads like him were very attached to the land; no wonder, I suppose, when they had stories like that to tell about every stone and every tree.

I was working (under the close scrutiny of Old Tim) for about half-an-hour when a van halted at the gate. It was the agent with the gelignite. He took a case from the back of the van and came to us across the field.

'Hello Pat. Where's this rock?' he asked me.

'It's over here,' John Patrick shouted abruptly. The two of us followed him. I glanced behind to see Tim's reaction. I had to smile. The way he was sitting erectly with his eyes open and alert he reminded me of a rabbit in that perplexed moment of terror after it sights danger and is deciding whether to stand or flee. Then he got up and followed us at a distance.

The agent surveyed the rock, looking all around it, standing back to assess its size and, finally, poking at its base. On one side of it grew the thorn bush that Old Tim was talking about. I wondered if there was anything to his story, if the rock really covered a grave.

'It will be easy enough to blow this,' reported the agent. 'A couple of sticks at the base should crack it open.'

He opened his case and took out two sticks of gelignite and a coil of fuse. He put the two sticks in tightly under the base of the rock; then attached the fuse and unrolled the coil.

'We'll take shelter behind that mound over there,' he said to us, and shouted to Tim: 'You had better get down well behind that mound, sir; there will be bits of rock whistling past your ears in a minute.'

John Patrick and myself got in behind the mound and called on Tim to do likewise. Presently the agent lit the fuse and came up to join us.

'Come on, old man, you have sixty seconds to get down,' said he to Tim. Old Tim stirred himself but, to our amazement, instead of coming behind the mound he made for the rock.

'Jesus, what's he doing?' cried the agent. I got up to run after him; but John Patrick grabbed me by the jacket.

'For Christ's sake, do you want to get killed too?' he roared.

I looked over the mound. Tim was approaching the rock and the fuse was still sizzling. He reached the rock and I saw him fumble about at the base. He took out the sticks of gelignite, held them in his hand and turned to walk away with them. At that I ducked my head into the earth and covered my ears with my hands. But I heard it, nevertheless, a dull boom. I was afraid to raise my head and when I did I was confronted by two faces which mirrored my own feelings: they were white with fear and dumb with disbelief.

I will not describe the scene that lay before us when we

approached the rock. It is sufficient to say that poor Old Tim was blown to bits and the rock, the Bleeding-Stone, undamaged, was drenched in blood and gore.

Even yet, and it is now years since the incident, I have not resolved the question that it posed to me. I have pondered it endlessly, turning it over in my mind, trying to analyse it, but I have never succeeded in breaking it down to rational terms; hence I have never reached a rational conclusion. I suppose that is the real nature of a mystery.

I need not add that the Bleeding-Stone is still there. Nobody has tried to move it since and I doubt if anybody ever will.

Estrangement

My brothers and I had cultivated the custom of rambling: each of us had a house in the neighbourhood which we patronised with regular and prolonged visits. Padraic, who was eighteen months older than me, rambled in Murphy's house, about a mile away, down near the sea; while my younger brother, Terry, visited Feeney's next door. We were the only children in the locality and the neighbours were mostly middleaged and unmarried; they were therefore glad of our company, while we luxuriated in the attention and hospitality that were lavished on us.

My own house for rambling was that of Charlie's Pat. He had always fascinated me. For a man whose name indicated that he belonged to someone, he was singularly alone and unwanted. His house had once been a three-room thatched cottage; but when the roof of the lower bedroom collapsed in a storm he made no effort to restore it: he just withdrew into the kitchen and upper bedroom; more recently the roof of the kitchen had collapsed, so now he was living in the one remaining bedroom.

That room was extremely cluttered. All the furniture that had once been distributed throughout the house was packed into it: there was a kitchen table, a double bed, a dresser, several chairs, a form, two large cupboards, and a host of smaller items. When I walked about I had to pick my steps carefully between saucepans, pots, pans, jugs and other objects that were disposed about the floor. I was always in particular dread of stepping into, or overturning, his white enamel chamber pot. Pat lived in that room day and night and was seldom seen abroad. Yet he had mysterious ways, for, although I never saw him go to the shop or to the village, every day that I visited him he gave me a three-penny bar of Cadbury's chocolate. No matter how frequently I visited him, or at what time, he always had the bar of chocolate ready.

Father maintained that Pat had plenty of money, for he was in America when he was young; but I could never believe that he had: Pat led a very austere life. Apart from the condition of his house, there was also the evidence of his clothes: he wore very old, very tattered clothes, and when the weather was cold he tied a potato sack around himself by way of an apron.

My rambling was essentially different to that of my brothers. Dan Murphy, who was a fisherman, often brought Padraic out in his boat, teaching him how to draw in the net or empty a lobster pot. Terry did messages for the Feeneys — Michael, Pat, and Kate — and helped them with the farm work. I, on the other hand, always sat in Pat's smokey room, holding conversation with him after the manner of an adult.

Whenever there was a rush of work at home and our services were required, rambling was proscribed. It always happened when the big seasonal jobs occurred, such as the planting of the potatoes, the footing of the turf, or the hay-making. It happened also one November when my brother, Fiachra, was coming home from England. There was a great bustle around the house as Mother ordered us about, washing and painting, cleaning and tidying.

Fiachra was the eldest of our family. For the previous five years he had been away in England where he worked in a pub at night and went to the University during the day. He had recently received a degree from the University, so he was making a triumphal return. Mother was very excited and Father went around smiling and chuckling to himself like a simpleton. But my brothers and I scarcely remembered Fiachra and he existed for us only as a figure in the daily conversation, or as a model of success held contantly before our unambitious minds. We felt frustrated, therefore, being chained to the house for the third consecutive day, and we grumbled in our captivity putting on an exaggerated display of discontent.

At last Mother relented, shouting: 'All right, you can go off for an hour, but be back here by twelve, be back here when the Angelus is ringing.'

Bounding out of the house we scattered in three directions. It was not far to Pat's house. A stile crossed from the road into his place and two clean stone walls led straight to the front door. I was particularly fond of the two derelict rooms because he kept their flag-stone floors swept clean and there was a feeling of occupation about them still, so that whenever I looked up I was always half-surprised to see the sky.

I knocked on the door of the room and as usual there was a shuffle inside before Pat opened it. By contrast with the roofless kitchen, the room was dark and close. Pat cleared a basin from one of the chairs and told me to sit down. He went to the cupboard, fumbled about and produced a bar of chocolate. I thanked him and proceeded to unwrap the silver foil.

'Well, you're the stranger,' said he as a comment rather than as a reprimand, and he sat into his own chair by the fire. 'How are they all over in your house?'

'Not too bad,' I replied. 'We're doing-up the house beyond. That's why I couldn't get away. Fiachra will be home the day after tomorrow.'

'The day after tomorrow,' he repeated. 'It seems as if it was only yesterday that he left.'

'It seems an awful long time ago to me. It's nearly five years.'

'It's not so long at all since he was cycling in the road on his way to school. And to think that he has a University degree now! Your father and mother must be proud of him.'

'They are. Sure they never stop telling us how well Fiachra did, and how we'll never get anywhere if we don't work.'

'Troth, then, they have a right to be proud of him. It's not everyone from these parts goes off and works his way through University', exclaimed Pat with a spark in his eyes and a touch of passion in his voice which were uncharacteristic of him. Lifting his pipe, he resumed in his usual tone, 'You tell me it was in a pub he worked.'

And we proceeded on a conversation that we had covered hundreds of times before. The same questions were asked again and the same answers given; every success of Fiachra's career was recounted, every relevant proverb quoted to do

homage to his exertions. How Pat never tired of these repet-
itions mystified me.

When I heard the Angelus pealing I had to hurry away,
promising him that I would come again as soon as I could.

* * *

Three days passed before I visited Pat again; but, for the first
time in all my years of visiting him, I had news to tell him,
strange and shocking news which I was burning to impart.

'Would you believe that Fiachra is a communist?' I asked
as soon as I had the bar of chocolate in my hands, and I
watched his face for a reaction; but Pat was imperturbable.

'I take it he arrived so,' said he in his habitual, matter-of-
fact tone which left me deflated, wondering if he was avoiding the issue.

'Yes,' I replied. 'He came on the five o'clock bus yesterday
evening. There was great excitement. We had a chicken for
the dinner. Last night a few people came in rambling. Father
took out a bottle of poteen and everybody got merry. It was
very good until Fiachra got into an argument with Uncle
Martin. They were talking about education or something like
that. I think Fiachra was a bit drunk from the poteen. He was
saying that poor people would never get the same education
as rich people until there was a communist revolution. Then
Uncle Martin asked him if he was a communist and he said he
was. There wasn't much singing or anything after that and
the people went home.'

'How does he look? He must have changed a lot since he
left home.' Pat again seemed deliberately evasive.

'I think he's changed a bit all right. But then I can't remember too well what he looked like before he went away.'

'He was always a fine cut of a lad, tall but a bit thin, I
expect he has filled out by this.'

There was a lull in the conversation while Pat was removing a pot of potatoes from the fire. I decided to try a more
direct approach. 'What's a communist anyway, Pat?' I asked
with an assumed innocence, knowing full well from the way
people reacted to the word that it must in some way be link-
ed with the devil.

'Well, it's hard to say.' Pat pondered a moment. 'Russia is a communist country, and people who are communists want this country to be like Russia. They have some kind of a system where the government owns everything and then each person can get or borrow whatever he wants off the government.'

'Is that all?' I asked incredulously. 'It seems daft to me.'

I couldn't understand what all the fuss was about. Why should people be so vehement about something as trivial as that? Pat wasn't able to enlighten me so we talked about the weather and the crops for the rest of that visit.

* * *

I did not see Pat again until Sunday afternoon. In the meantime the strained relationships at home had developed to a crisis. That morning Father was shaving himself and preparing for church. I heard him ask mother if Fiachra was going to mass. She replied that she didn't know.

'Well, if he wants to go on with that kind of blackguardism, he can go back to England where he learnt it,' shouted Father belligerently.

I was still in bed at the time. I looked across the room and saw that Fiachra was lying awake, staring at the ceiling. I wished he had never come home.

He lay there all morning and didn't get up for either mass. Father was extremely vexed and hurt. He wandered around the house in a brooding reticence, doing unnecessary chores with a scarcely restrained violence. I reflected on the contrast between his present mood and the joy with which he had been anticipating Fiachra's return. Again I wished he had stayed in England. To escape witnessing this crucifixion of Father I decided to visit Pat.

Besides, there were questions I was asking myself regarding Fiachra's behaviour, and I thought that a conversation with Pat might help towards answering them. For Pat never went to church, something I had not considered before. In fact I had never before been conscious of religion as a factor in the division of people.

'It's really bad over there today,' I explained to Pat.

'Fiachra didn't go to mass.'

Pat didn't answer, but he didn't change the subject either; so I took a deep breath and, with as much nonchalance as I could muster, I asked: 'How come you don't go to mass yourself, Pat?'

He glanced at me sideways with an expression which conveyed that I had touched the quick beneath his complacent exterior.

'You'd be too young to understand those things,' he replied. 'But I have my reasons. Don't think I haven't got my reasons.'

'Do you think that Fiachra was right not to go?' I asked.

'Well, I can't answer for Fiachra. He probably doesn't believe in religion; and if he feels strongly that he shouldn't go to mass, then I think he was entitled to stay away.'

'But even if he doesn't believe in it himself, couldn't he have gone just to please Father and Mother?'

Pat raised his voice and spoke emphatically with undisguised bitterness. 'The way I see it, it's a question of freedom. People are trying to make you do what they want, all the time. If a man gives in to them, then he gives up his freedom. And without his freedom a man is no better than a bullock penned up in the field beyond. The church is the worst of all for telling you what to do. If you gave in to that crowd, they'd have you looking for permission everytime you wanted to blow your nose. Fiachra is a young man with his life ahead of him. How he manages his life is his business and he's right not to let anyone tell him what to do.'

I said no more on the subject, for I didn't agree with Pat. I was disappointed in him. What had always appealed to me about him was his apparently easy-going attitude to life. But now I saw him in a different light. His inertia did not spring from a natural indifference to the world; he was as full of longing for life as the rest of us, but his outlook had crippled him with some sort of paralysis.

I felt very strongly that Fiachra should have gone to mass, while he was at home anyway. If he didn't believe in it, if it meant nothing to him, then it should have been a small thing to do to avoid making Father and Mother miserable.

And as for freedom what good did his freedom do Pat?

How much better off was he than the bullock penned into the field beyond?

* * *

A few days later Fiachra returned to England. We seldom heard from him after that. There was the occasional short letter, usually enclosing a postal order.

In an effort to compensate Father, who was depressed after Fiachra's departure, I took to attending mass daily. I gave up rambling in Pat's also: I wanted to spend more time working at home, or so I told myself. I often felt guilty, though, especially before I went to sleep at night, when I thought of the bars of chocolate growing mouldy in his cupboard. And sometimes in my sleep I dreamt that the inevitable had happened, that we awoke one morning to find the roof of Pat's last room collapsed and Pat smothered under the weight of the musty thatch.

Baptism of Water

8.30 a.m. The cars jerked and jostled slowly and ill-humouredly along Main Street. Down the deserted foothpath Mr. Joseph Cavanagh strode morosely past the shop fronts, their gaudiness faded by the morning light. Mr. Cavanagh thought of them as ageing whores: their painted attractions might be tolerable in an indulgent darkness but were repulsive in the merciless clarity of the dawn. This analogy occurred to him every morning since he first thought of it ten or twenty years earlier.

At the corner of William Street he had to step off the kerb to make way for three men staggering towards him evidently senseless from intoxication. Two of them were trying to carry their companion, his arms slung across their shoulders, their faces tightened in an expression of gigantic determination. He was rocking from side to side muttering drunkenly, "We'll die flying, like Daly's hen." Mr. Cavanagh paused to let them pass.

His habitual journey to school led him off Main Street and down the hill to the river. He never paused on this journey which took exactly twenty seven minutes. But on the first Tuesday of every month the cattle auctions in the town mart blocked the river-front with cars and trucks and trailers. Accordingly on the first Tuesday of every month Mr. Cavanagh was delayed on his journey and was late for school.

When he had picked his steps fastidiously over the green film of cowdung which covered the ground he stopped on the bridge, rested his briefcase on the parapet, and examined his shoes to ascertain whether he had preserved the immaculate shine his landlady had so conscientiously imparted to them the night before.

77

To his chagrin he found the toes smeared and even the tips
of his trouser-legs stained with the green slime. He took a
tissue from his pocket and tried to purge himself of the
odious filth, but without success. Mr. Cavanagh was deeply
vexed. Not only would he be late for school that morning
and have to face Moroney at the interview debilitated by feelings of guilt but his confidence would be further undermined
by an impaired self-image caused by the stain and stink of
cowdung.

The Headmaster had summoned Mr. Cavanagh to come to
his office at ten o'clock that morning. The subject of this
tete-a-tete was not communicated but Mr. Cavanagh knew
that, however it might be camouflaged with trivialities, the
important topic was the lack-lustre performance of his students in the public examinations.

Moroney would scratch his sleek head and comment on
the success of the school football-team and enquire how
rehearsals for the school opera were progressing, but sooner or
later he would open a gambit with a throw-away comment
such as, "I see your boys didn't do you justice in the Leaving."
And without accusation or condemnation he would proceed
to deliver a homily on the importance of examination results
and the precedence of English — "a key subject" or "a core
subject," depending on which cliche was in vogue with him.

Mr. Cavanagh gave up trying to restore the shine to his
shoes and tossed the tissue over the parapet into the river. He
watched it being borne swiftly away by a current which was
pulsing with vigour from the early Autumn rains.

Moroney would, no doubt, drop a few references to Finnegan, the President of the Board of Trustees, who was "keenly
interested in the welfare of the students". Mr. Cavanagh almost smiled. If Finnegan were anxious it would only be in
fear that he might somehow lose votes for the next Co.
Council election. A local shop-keeper, he posed as a "man of
culture", "a lover of the arts"; but his love of culture found
no higher expression than the purchase and consumption of a
bottle of French wine with his Sunday dinner.

Thoughts of Moroney and Finnegan made Mr. Cavanagh
weary, so weary he could have stretched himself out on the
ground.

I could lie down like a tired child,
And weep away the life of care
Which I have borne, and yet must bear,
Till death like sleep might steal on me.

The words of Shelley which he had ground into generations of students came into his mind. What irony that Shelley should be the grist for Moroney's mill, Finnegan's mill, yes and Cavanagh's mill — he could not deny the reality; he was no more than a drudge. In his own lifetime Shelley was hounded to death by their likes, just as he would be hounded to death now — an anarchist, a bigamist, an enemy of society. How nauseating that they should smile on him now and utter complimentary platitudes, they who would shrink in horror from what Shelley was advocating if they believed that anyone would take him seriously.

Mr. Cavanagh thought of a good comment for Moroney, one which he nevertheless knew he would not deliver: 'If I taught Shelley properly, Mr. Moroney, the boys would burn down the school instead of passing their Leaving Certificate.'

He looked at his watch. Already he was ten minutes late. The thought of turning back occurred to him declaring himself sick for the day. But no, that would be too cowardly. Why should he flinch before a pigeon-souled creature like Moroney?

Then he did an extraordinary thing. Standing on the bridge, resting against the parapet, he lit a cigarette. Mr. Cavanagh had never before paused on the bridge, not to mention loitering to smoke a cigarette. He inhaled the smoke stiffly but deeply and gazed down the river where it opened into a lough.

Shelley made the absolute protest when he drowned himself in the Italian sea. But his was the despair of the full man who could not persuade his people to share his vision. The despair of the empty man was different.

Mr. Cavanagh looked into the river and found it indeed seductive. It would be soothing to fill the void within him, even if it were only with water. It would be at least meaningful to die like Shelley in one final fierce gesture; in Mr. Cavanagh's case it would be the only gesture he had ever made. It would convulse the mean world of Moroney and Finnegan;

it would shake the youth out of their bland indifference; nothing would be the same, could be the same, afterwards. Or would it?

Perhaps his death would affect only one life — his own. Moroney would be annoyed at having to look for a new English teacher. The students would enquire if they were getting a day off as a result of the tragic event. The ripples on the water would fade away, and the accustomed state of tranquil torpor would be quickly restored.

Beneath the arches of the bridge the waters were gushing through, divided but not tamed by the abutments. Where the waters joined again they created little dancing whirlpools, angry little maws on the surface of the river. Round and round they spun, down and down, turning and sinking, ever converging upon their internal infinite.

Mr. Cavanagh saw as the greatest obstacle to suicide the loss of decorum involved in clambering over the parapet of the bridge, jumping fully-clothed into the river and perhaps, worst of all, shouting for help once he found himself in the water. And he imagined himself doing just that, regretting his decisiveness, struggling with the water, grasping after a shred of meaningless life, battling passionately to preserve an entity called Mr. Joseph Cavanagh. Yet it would probably be obvious, even then, even in that predicament, that Mr. Joseph Cavanagh had already died. Even if he reached the bank it would be a new Joseph Cavanagh that would pull himself out of the water. Washed away would be the old man stunted by years of mediocrity, dead the disgruntled teacher, drowned the ageing bachelor. And the new man born of water and impetuous action would go, dripping wet, to Moroney's interview and tell the little fat man that Shelley didn't write poetry so that boys could pass the Leaving Certificate or shop-keepers make polite conversation, but so that men could be free of their imaginary shackles. Then, reaching out, he would pluck one of his ears by way of resigning.

Mr. Cavanagh was feverishly excited by this train of thought. The possiblilty of new life far outweighed the risk of getting drowned. Yet the first obstacle was still insurmountable.

After a moment of perplexed thought a calm descended on

his agitated mind. He glanced around furtively and when he was certain that no one was observing him he took up his brief-case and flung it into the river. With mischievous delight he watched the brown leather bag float rapidly downstream. He imagined the copy-books within getting water-logged, the ink running over the pages and from one page to the next, making incomprehensible essays illegible, until 'A Day at the Seaside' was united with 'The Countryside in Winter' in one mass of sodden pulp.

When the bag finally disappeared into the distant lough Mr. Cavanagh looked at his watch. He would just be in time for his interview with Moroney. With the smug satisfaction of one who has just purchased a coveted object at a fraction of its normal price, he resumed his journey to school.

Conquest

As flies to wanton boys are we to the gods
They kill us for their sport.

(Shakespeare): *King Lear*

On a Saturday night in the middle of November Ivan Sweeney
left the house of a young girl on the main street. Ivan was a
notorious sensualist and generally had remarkable success
with women, but tonight he had failed. He was frustrated and
angry. If he had been younger he would have laughed at such
an eventuality and gone forth to try fate once more; but at
thirty he had little patience left and very little resilience.
Kicking the pebbles that lay in his path, he turned from the
main street and took a short-cut through the back alleys towards his home.

It was a frosty moonlit night; grey walls and concrete
sheds emerged out of the gloom as he walked along.

As he rounded a corner from one alley into another, Ivan
heard a loud caterwaul like the sound of a baby crying. He
stopped to listen. Then he tip-toed stealthily forward until he
saw a cat on top of a wall. She continued wailing, seemingly
unaware of his approach.

A queen in heat, thought Ivan, pausing to watch the cat;
tonight she's randy; three times in a year she gets the urge
and when she does she climbs up on a wall to let everyone
know she's dying for it. That wail must be penetrating every
house and backyard for miles. By now it's wakening every
tom cat in the neighbourhood, exciting him, telling him to
come and get it. Some of them have, perhaps, set out already,
climbing the face of a concrete wall, treading the glass-
crowned summit, tearing through a mesh of barbed wire:

they are driving forward in a frenzy of lust, their hearts pounding, pounding. Others are trapped in the parlours of respectable homes; nevertheless they hear and claw frantically at doors and windows. Yet, only one will have the satisfaction of copulating; only one will lie limp and sated.

It's not fair. It's not bloody fair. What about the others, the hundreds who have been roused out of their sleep by this senseless clarion to go pacing through the night with their brains on fire? What of the dozens imprisoned in the cosy sittingrooms?

The cat was sitting on her hindquarters, her back stretching upwards and her head tilted towards the sky. She was still wailing and had not yet detected Ivan's presence. Looking up at her he felt an intense hatred surging up within him: a shadow passed over his mind; a wish to destroy the whole female sex goaded him. He sprung at the wall and grabbed the cat by the neck with his left hand. She screamed and wriggled in fright. He passed his right hand around her neck from the front and squeezed with all his might; the cat's black body writhed baring her claws and striking vainly at the air. As he held her he was looking directly into the cat's face. Her round green eyes glared at him with ominous luminosity; like two circles of green fire they glowed at him in the moonlight. He tightened his grip on her neck and soon she was quite dead. But the eyes continued to glow. He clenched his hands in a vice-like grip, to no avail: the two green eyes stared resolutely at him as if they were defying him to quench their light. In a burst of fury he flung the odious body from him as far as he could over the garden wall.

In a state of nausea and depression Ivan proceeded homewards. However, the depression lifted even before he emerged on to his own street. For, sauntering towards him, he saw the figure of a young woman. As she approached he engaged glances with her, smiled and nodded, 'Goodnight'.

'Goodnight to you too,' she smiled back.

'Could you tell me if this lane leads on to Stephen's Street?' he enquired pleasantly.

'Yes. If you continue down the lane you will see Stephen's Street in front of you.'

'Thank you. You are kind. I wasn't quite sure. I'm on my

way to the "Falcon" public house. Could I take the liberty of inviting you to join me for a drink?'

She smiled again. 'No, thank you. I live here and at present my husband is away from home, so you can imagine the gossip if I were seen in a pub with another man.'

'That's a pity,' said Ivan, greatly disappointed.

'However,' she continued, 'if you would like to come back to my house, I could offer you some tea. There is nobody at home and the back entrance is only a short distance down the lane.'

'That would be very pleasant.'

As they walked back to the garden entrance, Ivan took stock of the lady's delights with the intense joy of anticipated pleasure. She appeared to be in her early twenties, with a well-proportioned figure; every step she took was a complete movement of her body from her toes to her forehead. He liked that; in fact he abhorred women who used their legs like stilts to prop-up and transport their bodies. Yes, Ivan was fastidious, but throughout his years of indulgence he could not have avoided acquiring a delicate palate.

She opened the back door and they passed through a small kitchen into a spacious and much-cushioned sittingroom.

'Please sit down.' She ushered him towards a large sofa, drew the curtains and switched on an electric standing lamp. 'I will make some tea.'

While she retired to the kitchen and busied herself with cups and kettle and running water, Ivan surveyed the sittingroom. His eyes raked the wall-hangings and numerous photographs in quest of a picture of her husband. There were some old photographs, brown and faded, of family groups; there were new ones too with photographers' sets and contrived postures. But not a single dominant one suggested its representing the master of the house. When she returned bearing a tray laden with crockery he enquired: 'Has your husband been away for long?'

'For months.' she replied dolefully. 'He's a sailor and his voyages are always long. At the moment he is probably in Hong Kong.'

I couldn't wish him much further away, thought Ivan amusedly, and certainly I wouldn't wish him any nearer.

"It must be very lonely for you while he's at sea,' he said sympathetically.

'Oh, I do my best to keep the boredom at bay, but it's no joke, I'll admit."

'He must have plenty of leave when he does come home.'

'It doesn't compensate for his absence, really. You see, he comes back with two months' leave and after a fortnight he's tired of loitering about, so he gets contrary, and the honeymoon atmosphere isn't long dispersing.'

She poured out the tea, handed him a cup, sliced some cake and held out the plate to him. He took the first slice which, being the end of the cake, was covered on one side with yellow icing; he was very partial to icing. She took the next slice and they sat eating, silent for a moment.

'I don't know your name,' she resumed presently. 'Mine is Pearl.'

Ivan was a little confused and embarrassed. Had he forgotten to introduce himself? He had. It was an important point, one that came early in his strategy — and he had omitted it. He was angry with himself. However, he smiled and nodded.

'Mine is Ivan.'

'Where do you live, Ivan?'

'I live in this neighbourhood, actually, just a few streets away.'

'It's odd then that I have never seen you before.'

'Yes, I've never seen you either,' replied Ivan. 'I suppose it's coincidence in reverse.'

She smiled at that and took another mouthful of cake. Ivan felt insecure, out-manoeuvred in a delicate matter, but he laboured to overcome this feeling as he knew that a sense of superiority was the indispensible pre-condition of a conquest. He studied her carefully. She was neatly lifting the cup to her lips while her black hair dropped forward on both sides of her face. Sitting in a low easy-chair her dress receded on her thighs and revealed a pair of beautifully moulded legs. Ivan's lust was roused and he was ready to take the offensive once again.

When they were finished eating she collected the cups, saucers and plates, stacked them on the tray and brought them back to the kitchen.

'Would you like to hear some music?' she asked on her return.

'Very much. May I see your records?'

She opened a mahogony side-board and took out some records. Ivan crossed the room to examine them. He turned over a few, Monteverdi, Beethoven; classical records mostly; he knew very little about classical music; eventually he picked out 'Segovia — Guitar Music.'

'How about this?' he asked, and with an interrogative gesture he raised his hand to catch her arm lightly. When he dropped his hand again, he let his fingertips trickle down her arm until they flowed into the pool of her curved palm. She pressed his fingers gently, then took the record and placed it on the turntable.

'I like Segovia,' she said.

'I do too,' agreed Ivan; in fact he had never heard Segovia's music but had remembered the name mentioned on a few occasions.

He put his arm around her waist and drew her back to the sofa. They sat closely and she leaned her body against him. Shifting his position so that she reclined on the back of the sofa, Ivan kissed her on the neck, then on the mouth. She responded passionately setting her tongue loose between his teeth.

Gently he lowered her until she was prone on the sofa, still kissing, pressing mouth against mouth in a rapacious intercourse of tongues. He ran his hand along her thigh, peeling her dress up to her hips; his fingertips tingled from contact with smooth silk. He pushed her dress up to her waist and felt the soft flesh of her stomach. Edging his hand down to her pelvis, his fingers combed through her pubic hair. That was odd! Instead of the wiry texture of pubic hair to which he was accustomed, hers was soft — almost furry. He thought of the cat, recalled the feeling of its neck between his fingers, the inextinguishable glow of its eyes. A cold sensation came over him causing a shiver along his spine. He withdrew his hand. His passion was cooling. Desperately he tried to think about the girl, to suppress the image that was freezing him to the core. But it was no use; his lust was forsaking him. The girl looked at him in surprise.

'Is there anything wrong?' she asked.

'No, it's just something that occurred to me,' he replied dejectedly. Two green eyes burned icily in his mind. 'Damn that cat', he thought, 'coming on me like that, spoiling the mood.'

'Don't you want to make love to me?' she persisted.

'Of course I do,' replied Ivan, endeavouring to muster a smile.

'Then come on.' And she began to undress.

Ivan watched her, trying vainly to revive his frozen eros. She was naked now, beautifully naked. Maybe if he stripped he could again arouse his desire.

'Come on,' she invited as she curled up on the sofa.

Somehow he felt defeated. Never before had he played the passive role. He undressed and went to her, but he could not banish the cold nervous feeling from his loins. It was aggravated by the awareness that she was expecting a standard of performance from him, that she was experienced, superior, and already judging him.

'Don't you find me attractive?' she complained presently.

'Of course I do; it's just that I'm not in form tonight,' stuttered Ivan unconvincingly.

'In that case, we'll call it off,' she replied in a huff and started to dress herself again.

Ivan also put on his clothes. Fully robed, he left without saying a word. But all the way home he muttered bitterly:

'Shag that cat; shag that bloody cat.'

Dunorlar's First Annual Festival of Satire

Never before had the town's Community Centre looked so well to our eyes. An array of drawings, paintings and water-colours enlivened the bleak walls. Sculptures in metal and stone punctuated the horizontal space across the wide floor. Two cubicles were erected in opposing corners, one to show 16mm films, the other to project a succession of slides on to a screen. Throughout the hall, with calculated abandon, pages and leaflets containing literary offerings were scattered. Everything had been thought of and everything was in order for the opening of Dunorlar's First Annual Festival of Satire.

* * *

FAUST — 20th Century

At the back of the shop
was a slot machine,
dirty and soiled
an oily green.

Those seeking to barter
came back here and read:
'Insert one soul
for a loaf of bread'.

* * *

We had thought it a weird idea when we first heard of it. The Town Council had had an extended discussion on how to boost Dunorlar's attractiveness as a tourist centre. The only scheme which the Council could think of was a festival. But

what kind of festival they couldn't decide; all the best ideas
for festivals had already been grabbed-up by other towns —
rather inconsiderately, it seemed to our town fathers. No way
out of this impasse could be seen until Tom Burns, a local
teacher of an eccentric turn of mind, suggested a festival of
satire. The rest of the Council members enquired eagerly if
the idea had been used in any other town. When they were
assured that it was a completely novel idea, a motion was
quickly passed to give Dunorlar the festival it needed so badly
to lure the natives out of the hinterland and the Germans out
of Hamburg.

* * *

* * *

Not surprisingly, it had been left to Tom Burns to organize
the satire for the festival, while the rest of the town got on
with the serious business of ordering up stocks of drink and
food and confectionery to cater for the expected deluge of
visitors.

Willie and I had long admired the style of Tom Burns, his
air of detachment and independence; so, when we heard of the
huge task he had undertaken, we volunteered to help him.
We were students at the Technical School where Burns taught

Mathematics but not, we regretted, to us.

The exhibits and entries for the festival started to arrive from all kinds of strange sources. We began to get excited about the whole project. There was material there which, we felt, was going to create quite a fluster in our conservative and sheltered little town. And we began to wonder about Burns's motives.

* * *

NEWS ITEM FROM A VETERINARY JOURNAL

Dr. Alfred Gut, who has been carrying out research under a fellowship funded by the R.S.P.C.A., claims he has now devised the ultimate humane rodent-exterminator.

Destined to make cruel traps and barbaric poisons obsolete, Dr. Gut's invention is a sweet powder which rodents find delectable, even irresistible. It operates as a highly effective abortifacient, which means that the present generation of rats and mice can live out their natural lives to a ripe old age, enjoying Gut's powder, but no replacement stock is born.

Immediate reaction from an R.S.P.C.A. spokesman was warmly enthusiastic. He stated: 'Thanks to Dr. Gut, we can now control our rodent population problem by being nice to our less fortunate fellow-creatures'.

* * *

The week preceding the opening was spent in a fevour of preparation. The hall had to be ridded of its bingo atmosphere and its tons of tatty furniture. Then we sorted out all the paintings and hung them on the walls. Tom Burns stood back, a pencil behind his ear, determining the exact location for each picture, while Willie and I hammered the nails.

Making the panels for the cubicles was the hardest job, especially as we had had to 'borrow' the timber and hardboard out of the builder's yard, and Sweeney, the storeman who had 'lent' it to us, looked painfully in the door every time he passed the hall to see what injury we were doing to his precious materials.

* * *

ODE FOR YESTERDAY'S WHISKEY
(With apologies to Thomas Moore)

At the rush-hour of eve, when cars are beeping, I fly
To the quiet pub I loved, when you were the light of my
eye;
And I think oft, if spirits could steal from the regions
below
To revisit past scenes of delight, from those sewers
you'd flow
And I would be merry again, and no one would know why.
Then I'd sing the wild song that I once with rapture
composed,
When my voice and your odour breathed like one on the
nose;
And as echo far off through the cellar my orison rolls,
I think, O my Drink, 'tis thy ghost coming up through
the holes,
To give me more value for the notes that I paid — and so
dear!

* * *

Early on that Friday evening of the official opening Willie and I were down in the hall checking and re-checking everything, admiring and re-admiring the exhibition, reading and re-reading the leaflets. The 16mm projector was fitted with a short Japanese film on the subject of pollution, called 'When there are No More Fish in the Sea'. It had come from the Embassy of Japan in Dublin. The other projector was loaded with slide-reproductions of Surrealist paintings. These had been supplied by some Art teacher that Tom Burns knew. Both projectors were functioning perfectly, much to our surprise.

At half-past seven we pulled back the wide doors. The official opening of the festival was timed for eight o'clock, and we expected the crowds to be gathering well beforehand.

It was nine o'clock and nobody, absolutely nobody, had yet turned up for our official opening. We were growing extremely anxious. We couldn't understand it because it was quite evident that the town had filled up with people. Most of all, we were worried on Tom Burns's account, that the Festival wouldn't be a success.

Willie had gone down to the take-away cafe and returned with two bags of chips. We sat eating them, pensively, in the splendour of that empty hall, the vinegar-steam rising up in front of a picture called 'A Modest Proposal,' in which the figures of famine-afflicted infants were garnished on a serving-dish, a gigantic knife and fork on either side. Tom Burns had explained to us how it was based on an essay by Jonathan Swift.

All this time Tom Burns had been drifting about the exhibition, now sitting down to watch the slides, now re-reading some of the literature. But he appeared totally calm and unconcerned. This was re-assuring to us.

* * *

INSCRIPTION ON A CONFUCIAN LOO

*The man who looks into his own heart and finds
no evil there is simply not looking hard enough.*

* * *

At ten o'clock the Chairman of the Town Council arrived to perform the opening ceremony. His wife was at his side, heavily made-up and dressed in vulgar imitation-fur. When the Chairman saw the empty hall he was visibly taken aback. Yet it was obvious that his dismay was caused not so much by the outrageous lack of public support as by the prospect of no one hearing his specially rehearsed speech. He stood, looking awkward and fidgeting, for a few minutes. Eventually, he muttered to Tom Burns: "The best thing to do is go down to Kelly's Hotel. They have a big crowd down there for the dance. Packed it is. I passed it on my way up. We can hold the official opening down there.'

The Chairman went off down the street, with his wife at his side.

Tom Burns walked slowly around the centre of the hall, taking one last look at the exhibition before leaving. Suddenly he burst into a convulsive fit of laughter, a laughter that was full of mirth, full of knowing. And we laughed too, because Tom was laughing, and because we felt we were beginning to understand something.

'Put out the lights, boys,' said he at last, 'and we'll go and witness the official opening of our Festival of Satire.'

* * *

A FABLE ASCRIBED TO AESOP BUT GENERALLY
THOUGHT TO BE A FORGERY OF RECENT ORIGIN

There was a lion in the jungle who was so mild that he would not hurt a fly. Such was his reputation for timidity that the rabbit and the hare would come and play hide-and-seek in and out among his four powerful paws.

Once while he was enjoying a nap in the sunshine he turned over and rolled by accident into a furze bush. A big sharp thorn stuck into his side and lodged there. The lion woke up in agony. He rolled over and over to try and shake off the thorn, but to no avail; he merely drove it deeper into his side. The pain was so intense that he let out a gigantic roar and set off at a gallop through the jungle. All the animals, who heard that blood-curdling roar and saw the lion rampaging fiercely, were terrified, and scampered into hiding.

The lion ran about the jungle roaring and snarling and before the day was out he had acquired a reputation as the fiercest lion in the whole jungle.

Eventually, the lion came across his little friend, the mouse, and persuaded him to pull the thorn out of his side. As soon as the thorn was extracted the pain began to subside, and the lion felt all his anger and fierceness drain likewise away. A short while later when the rabbit and the hare returned to play hide-and-seek in and out among his four powerful paws, the lion began to regret the departure of his anger and his fierceness. Then to his slow reason occurred the conception that it was the thorn in his side which had caused his fit of rage and had momentarily enforced the respect of the whole population of the jungle. This led to a deduction: if he had just a few thorns in his side, he could even become the fiercest lion in the whole world.

So he galloped back to where the furze bush was growing, and he charged into it. When he re-emerged he was covered all over with thorns. There were thorns in his side, thorns in his legs, thorns in his great mane, thorns everywhere. Shortly afterwards he died of blood-poisoning.

MORAL: *A thorn in your side may prove a useful stimulus, but too many thorns in your side can give you a pain in the arse.*

* * *

Walking a few paces behind Tom Burns, down the long main street, we felt as if we were seeing the town for the very first time. There were crowds packed into every pub, and every pub in the town had secured an extension of drinking hours for the duration of the Festival.

Kelly's Hotel was crammed and we had to elbow our way into the huge lounge at the back where the dance was taking place. We arrived just as the Chairman was trying to impose silence on a noisy and uninterested audience. We caught phrases of his speech over the din, 'great honour,' 'Festival a marvellous success', 'hard work', 'tribute to Town Council'.

Eventually he seemed to tire of his efforts and he got down off the bandstand without notice or ovation. The band struck up a quickstep and a horde of people struggled into the little square of timber floor.

THE COWS AND THE YELLOW MOON

I looked
in my sweetheart's eyes
when the yellow moon was rising:
my love
     was
        a yellow moon
my love was a flash of lightening.
the earth was covered
           with cows
and the cows were eating grass,
I sang a song about love
but the cows
       were eating
          grass;
I cried aloud
       to the cows
to look up
to jump over
      the moon
but the cows never lifted their horns
they were busily
        busily
         eating
           grass.

The Land of Dwarfs

for Henry J. Sharpe

PROLOGUE

The Book of Mion

Chapter One

1. *Fleeing before the persecuting forces of the Empire, Mion and his nine followers sailed their raft into the arms of the wind and surrendered themselves to fate. They were blown swiftly in the direction of the dying sun. In three days they reached an island and put ashore.*

2. *The coastline was rugged where great mountains slopea precipitously into the sea. Scouting along the shore they found no sign of habitation nor the means to sustain it. They resolved, therefore, to scale the mountain range and inspect the other side.*

3. *On reaching the crest of the mountains, Mion and his companions beheld the great central plain of the island, stretching on every side towards encircling hills. The plain was lush with meadows and woods and displayed abundant evidence of cultivation.*

4. *Weak with trepidation and despair, his followers beseeched Mion to proceed no further, for they feared an encounter with the natives. Being dwarfs, they had suffered torture and*

degradation in their own country, and they expected no better treatment from the inhabitants of this island.

5.   But Mion exhorted them saying, 'What have we to lose, brothers, but our lives? And what are our lives worth in our present plight, outcast from our own country, hungry, weary of the long journey? Is it not better to try our fortune with these people than to turn to the sea again?*

6.   *Reluctantly they banished their fears and wound their way down to the green meadows and the rolling pasture land. On every side there were thorn bushes and fruit trees in full bloom.*

7.   *Eventually they came to a place where a group of farmers was tilling a field. They were digging in the primitive fashion, with mattocks and spades.*

8.   *When they saw Mion and his followers they fell into consternation and cried out 'Luchorpain,' 'Luchorpain'. Even though they were twice as tall as the dwarfs they were trembling in awe and terror.*

9.   *Mion raised his hands in a gesture of friendship. 'People we come here in peace, not in hostility. Let us be friends. There is much we can teach you. Fetch me an ox and some ropes. Hand me an axe.'*

10.   *Cutting down a tree, Mion fashioned a rough plough-share. When the ox was brought he improvised traces and tackled the ox to the ploughshare. With the ease of walking Mion drove the ox down the field, cutting a long deep furrow as he went.*

11.   *On seeing this the farmers were even more amazed. They took off their caps and bowed down before Mion and the other dwarfs. Again they muttered 'Luchorpain', 'Luchorpain'.*

12.   *'What do you mean by 'Luchorpain?' asked Mion. The*

farmers replied, 'We have often seen you in our dreams and witnessed your magical powers. Then we called you by that name.'

13.   *The farmers entertained Mion and the nine with hospitality, giving them food and shelter and an honoured place at their table.*

Chapter Two

1.   *When he was alone with his companions, Mion addressed them, 'What an auspicious country we have come into, my brothers. In our homeland we were treated with ridicule and hatred; here we are greeted as if we were supernatural beings.'*

2.   *'You have witnessed that our coming has been foretold to these people in their dreams. Let us think about that, my brothers. Who has access to the mind of man and can plant the seeds of thought therein? None but a god!'*

3.   *'And if god has been so partial towards the form of the dwarf, he must have some reason for this partiality. It is because god himself is a dwarf and therefore holds sacred all who partake of his own form.'*

4.   *'It is the manifest wish of the Dwarfgod that we throw aside our old opinion of ourselves. We must dedicate ourselves to his cause and ensure that he is always revered on this island.'*

5.   *'And since the form of the Dwarfgod must be the perfect form, it is our duty to mould the people of this island in his image and likeness.'*

6.   *On the following day a great crowd gathered. News of the dwarfs had spread, and all who heard wished to see the diminutive creatures with the extraordinary powers.*

7.   *Standing on a hillock, Mion spoke to them. 'We have been sent to you, O people, by the Dwarfgod, he who holds the lives of all men in the palm of his hand.'*

8.   *'He is angry with the people of this island for you have, of late, been lacking in your devotion to him.'*

9.   *'But before he punishes you, he has decided to give you one last chance. He has sent us to show you the true path to the throne of light.'*

10.   *The people trembled at the thought of incurring the wrath of the supernatural powers. They had always respected the holy places, but now they assumed that they had neglected some shrine of this new god.*

11.   *They fell upon their knees and raised their voices in supplication. 'Teach us how to make ourselves pleasing to your Dwarfgod. Do not leave us, o Luchorpain. Stay and show us the path of righteousness.'*

12.   *Mion answered them, saying: 'We will stay and lead you in the way of the Dwarfgod. But you must obey his law as we reveal it, for we alone have the gift of wisdom.'*

13.   *The people were relieved and accepted the dwarfs as divine emissaries, learning in time to obey them in all things.*

Continued

* * *

Aonar wandered alone on the slopes of the Boar Mountain. He knew every cave and boulder, every tree and stream on this mountain, for it was here that he was born and reared. He lacked companionship and so he studied the contours of this wild landscape as another might contemplate the features of a beloved.

There were a few people, mostly shepherds, inhabiting that mountain district; but they were invariably of the older generation, and they were always ill-at-ease when they spoke to him. For Aonar was different. Why he was different he did not understand; but, whereas his grandfather and the other shepherds were about four foot high with hunched shoulders and curled spine, Aonar was over six foot with broad shoulders and a back as straight as a pine tree.

At night, when he pretended to sleep, he heard his grandfather and the other shepherds whispering about him as they huddled about the fire with smoking pipes. They all seemed to agree that Aonar was cursed by the Dwarfgod. One old fellow related that before the coming of the dwarfs everyone in the island was like Aonar, tall and straight. But those were savage times, and the dwarfs brought civilisation — they banished the barbarous figure of the giant and everyone was blessed with the form of the dwarf.

The mystery which surrounded him weighed heavily on Aonar, and he was determined to find out the reason for his abnormality. If he was accursed, there had to be some explanation of the curse. He resolved, therefore, to confront his grandfather and elicit from the old man whatever information he could.

The grandfather was stopping sheep into a pen when Aonar found him. 'Grandfather,' said he, 'I need to have a long talk with you.'

'Certainly, son,' replied the grandfather. 'Help me draw the poles across and then we will go into the house.'

As soon as they were seated by the fire and the old man had his pipe lit, Aonar asked: 'Grandfather, why am I different to other people? I have heard it murmured that there is a curse on me. But why should I be accursed any more than another?'

The old man was surprised by the frankness of Aonar's questioning. He looked into the boy's eyes and saw there the earnestness and strength of manhood. There would be no putting him off this time.

'My boy,' he began. 'It pains me to have to unfold for you the story of your affliction. You are accursed, right enough, but it is not through any fault of your own. The guilt is partly mine, partly your mother's. For your mother committed the one unforgiveable sin, the one crime calling to the

Dwarfgod for vengeance: she bore you out of wedlock. The poor girl suffered for her sin: she died in the throes of child-birth. So you were left on my hands. I should have gone to the authorities and taken you to the special orphanage for illegitimate children. But the thought of my own shame being made public and the thought of the degradation to which you would be subjected tempted me to renege on my res-ponsibilities. Besides, in this remote corner of the island we never see an official, so who would know of your existence? I gave in to temptation. I did not register your birth, nor did I enrol you at the school. For these offences the Dwarfgod has seen fit to punish me. But the tragedy is that his bitter-est vengeance should be wreaked on you.'

'I wonder if there are any others accursed like me in the country,' said Aonar in a melancholy tone.

'I doubt it,' said his grandfather. 'The laws concerning illegitimacy and the laws concerning school attendance are the strictest in our land. The penalties for breaking those particular laws are extremely severe. I doubt that they are ever broken.'

Knowledge of the truth did not lighten Aonar's burden of loneliness and depression. He left the cottage and went out on the mountain slopes again, heading for the most secluded place he knew, Temple Wood. It was situated in a little dip or valley between two ridges and was dense with trees. So in-tense was the feeling of loneliness which Aonar always exper-ienced in this place that it actually purged him of all lone-liness and left him with a peaceful sensation, approaching joy.

But this time his agitation caused him to climb and clamb-er more deeply into the wood than he had ever gone before. In the matted interior he found, to his delight, a stream which he had not discovered previously. He followed the course of the stream down the bed of the valley. Presently the trees parted and the stream flowed through a beautiful glade. There were grassy banks on either side and the trees stood clear in a wide circle.

Aonar was excited by this discovery. He threw himself on the grass letting the filtred rays of sunlight warm his whole body. Lying there, watching squint-eyed the almost-trans-parent leaves being blown in the wind high above his head, he whispered to himself that he was the first person ever to set foot in this glade.

He glanced at another tree further away and what he saw made him spring bolt upright. He thought he saw a man perched like a squirrel in the topmost branches. Aonar shaded his eyes with his hand and advanced slowly to get a closer look. Sure enough it was a man, an old man with dishevelled hair and white beard. It took Aonar quite some time to recover from his surprise. The man did not move and Aonar wondered whether it would be proper to disturb him. Eventually his curiosity overcame his bashfulness and he addressed the stranger.

'Excuse me, sir. What are you doing up there?' Aonar asked as politely as he could.

The old man turned his head slowly and glared down at Aonar with all the brooding imminence of a thunder cloud. In a voice that came wheezing from his chest he replied: 'I am talking to my friends.'

'But I can see only you.'

'The world is full of blind people, so you are not exceptional,' retorted the stranger.

'I thought I was all alone. I didn't imagine I would meet anyone in the middle of this wood.'

The old man's glaring softened into an expression of surprise and then a flicker of curiosity seemed to light up his countenance. After a moment of silence he descended from his perch with an agility which belied his appearance of decrepitude.

'Let me see,' said he, examining Aonar thoroughly. 'I know. You haven't been to the school.'

'Yes,' replied Aonar. 'You see we're very isolated up here, and we're not always aware of what we should do.'

'It's all right. You don't have to explain, or apologise, to me. In fact I find you very interesting. I have never seen a fully-grown giant before.'

'Why are you out here alone?' enquired Aonar, anxious to divert the conversation before the old man asked any questions.

'I'm a hermit, and a hermit lives in the wilderness, doesn't he?'

'But what do you do out here?'

'I see sights. I hear sounds. I dream dreams.'

'Can you foresee the future?' asked Aonar.

The hermit laughed. 'It requires no gift to foresee the future. The future is always like the present, always like the past.'

'What a curious man you are,' said Aonar, warming to the stranger who all the while had been scrutinising him intently. 'My grandfather tells stories of hermits who explore heaven and hell in their weird dreams.'

'The fact is that everyone has wonderful dreams. People's dreams are never mediocre — their minds are. They fail to grasp the wonder in an intuition. That's the only difference between the commonplace man and the mystic.'

'But I cannot remember having had an interesting dream in my whole life.'

'Nonsense,' delcared the hermit. 'Come, you can sup with me and lodge tonight in my cell. In the morning you will relate your dreams and I will interpret them for you.'

Aonar was happy to accept the invitation. His experience and knowledge of life was so limited that he welcomed such an opportunity to learn. The hermit led him through the dense undergrowth until they came to a cave. They went inside and Aonar saw that it was beautifully adapted for living purposes, though it retained its natural frugality.

At the back of the cave was a shelf of rock and on it the hermit had books and manuscripts laid out. There was an array of writing quills and coloured inks. It was evident that the hermit was writing or copying the volumes that were stacked on the rock-table. Along one side of the cave was his bed which consisted of a hide thrown over a bundle of dried grass. Along the other side he had arranged his cooking utensils and his store of food. He took bread from a timber box and offered some to Aonar. They ate bread and drank water. When they had finished, the hermit produced a second hide and spread it on the ground as a bed for his guest.

In the morning the hermit shook Aonar to waken him, and said, 'Come tell me your dreams before they sink again into the depths of your mind.'

'Yes, I did have a curious dream,' said Aonar rising on his elbow and rubbing the sleep from his eyes. 'I dreamt that I was on the side of a mountain and below me there was a great pass. Through the pass there was a narrow but level path and along the path trudged an unending line of people in single file. The people did not greet me or acknowledge my presence, but plodded along slowly with eyes bent on the path before them. I walked beside them until the path widened where the mountains receded. Then ahead of me I saw a great dragon huge and fierce. The people kept walking forward completely unaware of the dragon, and the great beast devoured them one by one.'

'Then I felt something in my hand, and looking down I saw that I was holding a wonderful sword. Beautifully fahioned, it had a blade of the sharpest steel and a golden hilt studded with jewels; everywhere it was decorated with an intricate pattern of tracery. Somehow I knew that only this sword could kill the dragon. I advanced toward the monster slicing the air with long swishing strokes. The dragon, frightened, retreated step-by-step as I advanced. I attacked it from the side and soon it was trapped against the mountain wall. I moved in and raised my arm for the final blow. But suddenly my eyes blurred and changed focus; I saw in front of me, not a dragon, but a crowd of little men, cowering in terror of my blow. I dropped the sword in amazement; and again it was the dragon I saw.

'At that moment another young man appeared at my side, who looked at me with cold, scornful eyes. He took up the sword, raised, and struck the dragon right in the centre of its head. It fell dead at his feet. Still looking scornfully at me, he threw back the sword at my side from where he had picked it. I stared at him for a long time, and while I was staring, I witnessed a horrible metamorphosis: the young man's eyes grew red and fierce, and his skin became rough and scaly — he had become the dragon.'

'Do you know what the dream means?' enquired the hermit.

'I cannot explain it,' replied Aonar, 'and yet the significance of it is weighing against my mind like the pressure of a great lake against a dam.'

The hermit paused for a while and then spoke: 'It is not difficult to interpret your dream. The dragon you have seen is the dragon of institution. Institution is a predatory monster, all the more terrible and dangerous because it is intangible. It can take different shapes and different colours, and cannot be isolated from the victims it possesses. Never can it be annihilated. Like a ghost it takes possession of men, and will be exorcised from one only to re-possess another. As you saw in your dream, when it is killed it will grow again, even in the hearts of the very men who have killed it.'

'It is my destiny to fight the dragon, is it not?'

'Take the dream as a warning and avoid your destiny. It is futile, as you have seen, to try and fight the dragon. And nothing displeases the monster more than an unwilling victim. Give it the least opposition and your fate will be a thousand times more terrible than that of the succumbing masses.'

'I can see that you know the dragon in all its guises. Tell me where it is to be found,' said Aonar.

'Wherever you find an organisation superceding the people who comprise it, there you will find the dragon. Wherever you find people being limited by a creed, there you will find the dragon. Wherever you find conformity being valued above freedom, there you will find the bloated dragon grazing. In this country we have our native dragon in the form of the Petit Order of Dwarfs.'

'What is the Petit Order of Dwarfs?' asked Aonar.

'You really are ignorant of the ways of the world. The Petit Order of Dwarfs is the political and religious institution which rules this island. But, evidently, its rule doesn't extend this far. Have you never heard of Mion and his "little order"?'

'I'm afraid not,' replied Aonar embarrassed.

'Can you read?' enquired the hermit.

'Yes, my grandfather taught me to read.'

'Then I will let you read the "Book of Mion" which I am in the course of writing. In it you will find all things that have happened since the coming of Mion to this island.'

'I would be very eager to learn,' replied Aonar. 'But this morning I must return to my grandfather, as he will be anxious. May I return tomorrow to read your "Book of Mion"?'

'Tomorrow or any time you please.'

His grandfather was waiting for Aonar in a very agitated state of mind and he questioned him brusquely about his absence.

Aonar replied: 'Grandfather, the time is coming when I will have to leave this house forever, so it is best that we prepare for it.'

'What do you mean, "leave this house forever"? You can't go anywhere. Do you realise that you would be put to death immediately you were caught abroad?'

'Death may be my portion, Grandfather, but a death which has meaning is preferable to a life which has no meaning at all.

The old man was disturbed by these words, but could think of nothing further to say, and they both went about their accustomed tasks in more than usual silence.

Every morning, after his tasks were done, Aonar visited the hermit's cave to read through the volumes of the 'Book of Mion'. While he was reading, the hermit sat at the great stone, writing.

Aonar learned that all the inhabitants of the island had been giants before the coming of Mion. When the dwarfs came they took on themselves the complete government of the island. They built a palace for themselves. They raised a temple to dedicate the island to the Dwarfgod. Then they built a school so that children could be taken and moulded in the image of the Dwarfgod. Around these three buildings grew the Capital.

To ensure that their work continued after they themselves were gone, Mion and his followers founded the 'Petit Order of Dwarfs'. Only natural dwarfs — those favoured with the sacred form of the dwarf from birth — were eligible for membership of the Order. The Petit Order carried on the work of Mion efficiently from one generation to the next. So successful was the conversion to dwarfhood that within a few generations the height of the population had dropped miraculously and everybody partook of the sacred form.

On the night that he had finished reading 'The Book of Mion' Aonar lay awake until dawn, thinking. He had not read the complete book, only the volumes that were already written: even at that very moment the hermit was scratching out another volume. He remembered his dream of the dragon, and he realised that his fate was inevitable, as inevitable as the next volume of 'The Book of Mion'.

Whether to contend with the circumstances which life and his own nature imposed upon him, or to withdraw skulking in the mountain wilderness, that was his choice. And to Aonar there was no choice. He would contend. He would go to the Capital and present himself to the people.

When morning came he arose and explained to his grandfather that he intended to set out for the Central Plain. The old man pleaded and wept, but could not dissuade Aonar. He longed to bless the boy, but he could not, since that would be to invoke the Dwarfgod. So he stood silently weeping while Aonar collected a few belongings and bade him farewell.

Aonar went first to the hermit's glade. The hermit was eating his morning meal at the mouth of the cave.

'I see you have brought a bundle on your back. Have you come to join me?' asked he.

'No. I am on my way to the Central Plain', replied Aonar.

'Are you seeking death so eagerly? Don't you know that they must destroy you? You are a giant, a terrifying figure. For generations the people of this island have believed that giants are evil beings. The propagation of the dwarf civilisation depends on that belief. So what do you think you can achieve, you alone against the self-interest of the powerful institution, you alone against the prejudice of a nation?'

'Perhaps I can achieve nothing,' assented Aonar. 'But if a seed of grass falls on a patch of earth and fails to grow, it leaves the patch bare. Similarly, if a man does not do what he is ordained to do, he leaves a gap in the scheme of things. You talk of death — but to stay here would be to die in a deeper sense of that word. So I must go to the Central Plain.'

The hermit put forward no further arguments, and continued eating in a pensive manner. Aonar sat down beside him. When the hermit had finished his breakfast he arose and went into the cave. Returning, he placed a bundle of clothes in front of Aonar.

'Try these on,' said he.

Aonar picked up the clothes and examined them. There

was a plain white mask and a heavy black gown. He put them on, but the gown reached only to his knees.

'Try walking on your hunkers,' suggested the hermit.

Aonar squatted and found that the gown flowed down to his ankles. He tried hobbling along while maintaining that posture; it was awkward and cramping, but not impossible.

'Do you not think that I would attract just as much attention dressed in this outlandish disguise?'

'That is no outlandish diguise. That is the uniform worn by the teachers at the school. I will send you with an introduction. You can pretend you were studying under me. I'm sure they'll give you a position. Teachers wear their uniforms at all times, so you have a chance of avoiding detection.'

And so Aonar stayed three days with the hermit practising to walk on his hunkers and learning as much as he could about the Capital, particularly the school. When he was ready to leave for the Central Plain the hermit wished him well, saying: 'When you get to the school give them this letter. Say that you are a student of Fearfeasa and that you wish to be apprenticed to the teaching profession.'

Aonar thanked Fearfeasa and bade him farewell.

He made his way through the mountains and when he was at last overlooking the Central Plain he decided to don his disguise. Standing there, he wondered if it was the same view of the plain that Mion had beheld when he crossed the mountains. Underneath his teacher's gown Aonar shuffled along. The peasants he encountered on the way were very polite and deferential; the trade of teaching evidently commanded much respect. There was no hardship for Aonar now, for people kept offering him food and lodging.

Eventually Aonar reached the Capital. The clustered redbrick houses and the crowds of people in the streets were strange sights to him. Here and there were statues of the Dwarfgod with lights burning around them. People knelt on benches in front of these shrines contemplating the statues. Coming to an open square in the centre of the Capital, Aonar immediately recognised on three sides the temple, the school, and the palace of the Petit Order. The temple was a massive building, gross and irregular, which dominated the little town. The palace and the school were not as huge as the temple, but they nevertheless towered over the puny dwellings of the ordinary citizens.

He went up to the door of the school and knocked confidently. The doorman took him in and introduced him to the dwarf in charge of hospitality. This dwarf was a very old, weak-looking creature and he looked at Aonar through dim, watery eyes.

'I have come from studying under Fearfeasa, the hermit of Boar Mountain, with his recommendation that I be given the position of apprentice teacher here,' said Aonar stoutly.

'Ah, you come from Fearfeasa,' repeated the old dwarf. 'And how is our former brother keeping? A strange fellow — but no real harm in him! You chose a good master, my son. Fearfeasa is a man of wisdom.' He spoke in a senile, disjointed manner. 'And you wish to work in the school. Well, I'm sure we have a place for you. It's not every young man nowadays that wants to be a teacher. But first I must get you a meal. You must be hungry. And I'll show you to one of the guest-rooms.'

For the rest of the evening Aonar was entertained at the school in accordance with the code of hospitality. He was given a meal and a bed for the night. In the morning the old dwarf called him and took him to be interviewed by the Chief Instructor.

Although the Chief Instructor was dressed in the teacher's mask and gown, Aonar sensed that he was young: he was radiating cold energy. 'We will accept you as an apprentice.' he said to Aonar, 'but you will be on probation for a year, and if you are not absolutely suited to the task you will be advised to take up some other appointment.' Aonar nodded his acceptance of this condition. 'Now that you are a teacher, you must wear your mask at all times, before students, with your fellow teachers and among the public. We are striving at all times towards making our instruction impersonal — not an iota of the teacher's personality should be communicated to the student. Remember, your work is the most important work that anyone can perform: you will be moulding little children in the image and likeness of the Dwarfgod.

With that the Chief Instructor took Aonar on a tour of the school. He opened a door and strode into the first classroom.

Aonar looked around and was horrified to see, everywhere, tiny children creeping, falling, learning to walk, all of them encumbered by heavy metal frames in which their bodies were clasped.

'You will understand,' said the Chief Instructor, 'that at every stage in our educational programme we give equal importance to the training of the mind and the body. We subscribe to the old proverb "a dwarf's mind in a dwarf's body". This is the infant room, catering for students aged three to four. As soon as the children arrive in the school they are fitted with the sacred cast because the bones and the spine are malleable in that formative stage. If you look closely you will see that even in the youngest of the children the spine has curled and the shoulders have already hunched.'

Leaving the classroom, the Chief Instructor continued: 'Of course you will not be allocated to the junior classes until you have gained considerable experience. You will start with one of the senior classes.'

He showed Aonar into one classroom after another. The picture was similar in each: the children had their bodies contained within metal frames, the frames for the older children being only slightly larger. They arrived at a classroom which catered for senior students. These were probably about thirteen to fourteen, but it was difficult to guess their age because their faces had a hardened expression of premature ageing.

'This is Alphonsus,' said the Chief Instructor, introducing the teacher in charge of that classroom. 'He will be your tutor for the first few months. You will start in this room tomorrow morning.'

Alphonsus greeted Aonar cordially; then the Chief Instructor led him out of the room again.

'That ends our tour of the school,' he said. 'Be ready to start tomorrow morning. You will get great satisfaction from your work here. No achievement can be more meritorious than this, since nothing gives greater pleasure to the Dwarfgod than the sight of little children being moulded in his image and likeness.'

Aonar thought of the sight which gave pleasure to the Dwarfgod: children hobbling about in an ungainly manner,

learning to walk without grace, their bodies being deformed
by the shackles of a grotesque logic. He was moved to anger
but restrained himself, and the indignation of his countenance was well concealed by his teacher's mask.

That evening Aonar rested behind the locked door of his
room. He had much to think about. It was now easy to understand the facility with which the population of the island had
been reduced to dwarfs. But what a strange twist of fate had
allowed himself to grow up into a giant!

Alphonsus, his tutor, was warm-hearted and Aonar soon
established a close relationship with him. Not that he would
have confided in his tutor, but he was able to collect information from him which would have been difficult to extract
from another of a less sympathetic temperament. And one
day, Aonar got around to the enigma which most puzzled
him, the attitute of the Petit Order to marriage and procreation.

'Why do the dwarfs of the Order never get married?'
he asked.

'Well,' said Alphonsus, 'the whole question of sexuality and
procreation is one that is central to the philosphy of the
Order. For a start, they are all natural dwarfs, not cultured
dwarfs, as you and I are. The greatest sign of approval that
the Dwarfgod can bestow on any man is his own sacred form.
One aspect of this form is that the means of procreation are
decidedly ineffective: the pelvis of the female is too narrow
for parturition and the sexual organs of the male seldom
develop to maturity. It is logical to assume, therefore, that
the Dwarfgod wishes his chosen followers to be celibate, and
indeed wishes all people to aspire to the state of celibacy.'

Aonar worked hard and studied assiduously under Alphonsus. He was hungry for knowledge and when he came
upon a problem he never rested until it was solved. One of
the advantages of being a teacher was that he had access to
the Archives, a massive collection of books and manuscripts
which was available only to selected persons. Rich and
labyrinthine was the knowledge locked away in the great
tomes of the Archives. Most interesting to Aonar was the
section containing the records of the civilisation which
flourished on the island prior to the coming of the dwarfs.

There were thousands of stories in verse and prose extolling the feats of a tall and powerful people, stories of heroes who fought whole armies single-handed in defence of the island, stories of beautiful maidens whose red lips struck lovers dumb, stories of kings whose wisdom and justice were a by-word among the people. Aonar identified himself with the characters in these stories; it was as if he were the last descendant of that noble race. Yet it was not so; everybody on the island was heir to that tradition, and was born with the potential of becoming a giant. It was the school and the conditioning of the dwarfs that stunted them.

As time passed Aonar became more and more determined to sabotage the programme of deformation. But the only place where a person could stop the process was in the very place where the process began — the infant room. He would have to wait until he was allocated to that room before he could do anything.

The vision of children growing unencumbered excited him intensely, and he worked and studied even harder so that he would be noticed and promoted to the more responsible positions. Luck was on his side. He was only three months training under Alphonsus when he was given a class of his own. Six months later a vacancy occurred in one of the infant rooms, and nobody was surprised when Aonar was picked because he had become generally admired for his dedication.

He was now in the position he wanted, a room to himself with complete responsibility for a class of infants.

On the first day the Chief Instructor came in to show Aonar how to fix the cast to a child's body. The cast consisted of an upper piece, shaped to rest on the shoulders with an opening for the neck, and a lower piece which girded the hips and contained two openings for the legs. Four straight bars secured the two pieces to each other. The frame of the cast could be adjusted at the base of the bars — in the case of infants it was necessary to make an adjustment at intervals to allow for permitted growth.

There, in the cast itself, Aonar was amazed to find the answer to his problem. All he had to do was adjust the frame in advance of growth so that there would be no curtailing of the natural development of the child. He almost danced with delight when he saw how simple, yet how effective, his action could be.

For several months Aonar adjusted the frame of each child's cast so that he could grow uninhibited. Those who had been in the cast previously displayed a natural capacity to recover a straight back, and the new ones grew at a phenomenal rate. Whenever they had dreams of giants, as they frequently had, Aonar told them how lucky they were, that those were good creatures who would look over them and protect them in their sleep. (He had been instructed to use every opportunity of emphasising to the children that giants were evil savages.)

It was a time of intense happiness for Aonar; he knew he was doing what he was born to do. Yet it was a time of anxiety also; he feared that he would be detected before his work had a chance of being effective. He loved those children. Their faces and their individual quirks of personality were stamped on his mind. Even when he was alone in his bedroom their images were before him. And in his more sombre moments, Aonar realised that the time was coming when he would be no longer there to help them. He hoped that, when the hour of doom came, he would continue to live in and through these children.

Day followed day and no one suspected Aonar. He kept his. group of children isolated as much as possible and puckered the clothes around their shoulders to simulate a hunch.

But the day arrived when the Chief Instructor came around for a routine thorough inspection of the children. Removing the clothes from the first child to examine the progress of its training, he gasped with horror when he saw the child's back. He stared at it uncomprehendingly. Turning around he looked into Aonar's eyes, and then he understood. Hurriedly he examined the next child and the next and the next. Satisfied as to the extent of the sabotage, he ordered Aonar to follow him outside. In a fit of temper he tore off his mask and gown, only to be more amazed at the sight of the crouching giant.

Aonar felt embarrassed when he was uncovered squatting before the Chief Instructor. He stood up, stretching his cramped legs, and revealed his full height. The surprised

dwarf stood back gaping at him, but quickly recollecting himself he roared down the corridor and several teachers and
porters came running. All were astonished at the sight of
Aonar. The Chief Instructor shouted orders, and grabbing
the giant they marched him out of the school. They proceeded across the corner of the Square to the Palace of the
Petit Order. There he was handed over to the guards who
took him inside and committed him to a small, windowless
cell.

In the following hours many people peered in at Aonar
through the spy-hole in the door. There seemed to be much
commotion and much debate. Food was brought late in the
evening and, since it was evident that his fate would not be
resolved that night, Aonar lay down on the makeshift bed. In
spite of the predicament he was in, he had a contented mind
and as he fell asleep he ruminated happily on the children he
had rescued from a dreadful destiny.

The following morning Aonar was wakened early and led
from his cell by a guard. He was escorted along a maze of
corridors and into a large room where he was confronted by a
very officious-looking dwarf sitting behind a raised bench. On
either side of him were two clerks. Aonar was told to sit on a
chair which was placed in the middle of the room facing the
bench.

'What is your name?' asked the magistrate.

'Aonar.'

'Where do you come from?' How do you explain your
uncultured body?'

'I come from the region of the Boar Mountain,' replied
Aonar, 'and I grew up beyond the jurisdiction of your laws.
Although you can impose your creed on men, you cannot im-
pose it on nature; still less can you impose it on god.'

'You are a most impudent and audacious creature. We have
discussed your crime all night, and the nature of your punish-
ment. There has been no case like yours for many generations.
The recommended penalty is death. But we have decided not
to impose that penalty. Instead you will be banished from
the Capital and a proclamation will be issued forbidding anyone to give you food or drink, shelter or comfort. Nobody
will speak to you, so that you will wander the earth like a

homeless cur, an example of what it is like not to be a dwarf.'

'I care not for your penalties,' replied Aonar. 'For I have done what I came to do, and before long I will not be alone walking the highways. The fifty children that I have freed from your shackles will be joining me.'

'What pernicious rubbish you speak! What you have done to those unfortunate infants is brought them pain and distress, and nothing more. The process of moulding a child in the image of the Dwarfgod is painless if commenced, as it normally is, at an early age. Sometimes, for one reason or another, a child might be older when commencing; then its bones are hardened, and it has to undergo a special programme which is both painful and tedious. So you have not prevented these children being moulded in the image of the Dwarfgod. You have merely inflicted immense suffering on them, and they will curse your memory for the rest of their lives.'

Aonar's spirit was totally squashed. He had not thought that the system would be so relentless. If they regarded the normal programme as painless, what must the painful one be like? In his mind he saw his children writhing and screaming in some unimaginable torture chamber, and in their cries he heard his own name being cursed. What had he done to them?

He was so dazed that he was unaware of being dismissed by the magistrate and shown to the door. When he came to his senses he was out on the street. Passers-by were stopping to stare at him. Within minutes he was the centre of a circle of curious onlookers. He walked distractedly across the square, wondering what he should do. There was no hope in his soul. He was desperate.

When he reached the steps of the Temple he looked back and saw that a large crowd had gathered around him. He would have to talk to them; he would have to try and persuade the people, now, without delay. It was the only hope of saving the children. So he addressed the crowd:

'Why do you stare at me in amazement, o people. What you see is what you would have been had you not been processed by the school of dwarfs. Look at your bodies, o people, poor, ugly, stunted, twisted bodies that cry out against the desecration to which they have been subjected.

It is the dwarfs who are guilty of this desecration. They have conditioned your minds to accept as truth everything they say. But ask yourselves honestly, is it right to deform your bodies so?'

A young man stepped forward and replied: 'We do not agree that our bodies are deformed. Our bodies are cultured and moulded in the image of the Dwarfgod, which is the perfect form. Yours is barbaric and unsanctified.'

In reply Aonar unclasped his gown and threw it aside. He stood before them naked. 'I challenge any one of you to strip himself, so that we may judge which body is more beautiful, more supple and more powerful.'

There was an outcry from the people. Under the laws of the Petit Order it was forbidden for anyone to uncover his body in public. There were shouts of 'Sinner', 'Barbarian', 'He insults the Dwarfgod'.

'I am proof of a greater god than your Dwarfgod,' declared Aonar. 'I am proof that your Dwarfgod and your civilisation are false. Any creed that diminishes people is false and must be overthrown.'

A frenzied rage gripped the people. They surged forward and seized Aonar. They dragged him across the Square to the centre where trees were growing. Lashing his body to a trunk they nailed his hands and feet to the living timber. For three hours they left him there, slowly dying. After the initial storm of anger had passed the people stood around silently. Others gathered from far and near to watch the spectacle of the bleeding giant. Finally the last drop of blood drained from his body.

A member of the Petit Order, who was keeping the incident under surveillance, sensed a touch of melancholy in the atmosphere. He quickly announced a special ceremony of thanksgiving and the people followed him into the Temple.

EPILOGUE

The Book of Mion

Chapter 369

1.   The giant's body hung in the Square for three days. People came again and again to look upon it with fascination. A teacher named Alphonsus was said to have been seen weeping at the sight.

2.   When it was perceived by the Order that the spectacle of the crucified giant was far from having the anticipated effect, the body was taken down during the hours of darkness and buried, without ceremony, in an unmarked grave.

3.   But there was grumbling in the Capital. Some said that the giant had been badly treated, and malcontents in the Market Square began openly to criticise the Petit Order itself.

4.   One month after the death of the giant a group of youths marched to the Palace and demanded that the Archives be open to all who wished to study the civilisation of the giants.

5.   When it was feared that riots would break out in the streets of the Capital, an announcement was made that the President of the Petit Order, the living representative of Mion, would address the congregation in the Temple on the subject of the giant.

6.   On the day appointed people crammed into the Temple to hear the President's address. He said: 'The contentment of our lives has recently been disturbed by the unhappy intrusion of a doomed man, doomed not by us, but by his birth and the manner of his rearing.'

7.   'We did not raise a hand against him, even though his crime against our innocent children was great. No, it was the

people who rose up in righteous indignation when they heard their Dwarfgod reviled. It was the people who took the giant's life.'

8.   *'But this is not a time for bitterness or recrimination. And so we have decided to mark the passing of the giant with a monument at the spot where he died. The monument will be built, not by the customary subscription; it will be completely paid for by the Petit Order.'*

9.   *'And we will ask our sculptors to portray, upon the face of the statue, the loneliness, the despair of this man who was reared in the wilderness, without the blessing of culture.'*

10.   *'We will tell the sculptors not to refrain from depicting a certain savage beauty in the figure, because it will always stand as a reminder to us that if uncultured man is capable of some virtue and dignity, then the cultivated man, who has the blessing of the Dwarfgod, is capable of a million times more.'*

11.   *The people were deeply moved by the President's speech and they wept tears of pity for the unfortunate giant. They nodded gravely at the propriety of building a monument to him.*

12.   *There was dissension among the malcontents in the Market Square. Some said that they should build their own monument to the giant. Others held that they should contrive to demolish the Petit Order's monument as soon as it was built. While a few questioned the integrity of the giant himself for having an official monument erected in his honour.*

13.   *But before long the discord quietened, the emotions mellowed, and only the statue remained to remind people of the strange creature who had come down from the mountain with the intention of subverting the institutions of the island.*

Continued

Gelding

You asked me whether sexuality is a bridge or a barrier between man and woman. I don't know the answer. Who can say? Who can be dogmatic about anything in this life?

But your question resurrected a strange memory of an old experience, raised it like a ghost from a long-since landscaped cemetery; and, like a Lazarus summoned from his slumber, it has been haunting me ever since, loitering aimlessly at my shoulder, waiting perhaps for an explanation as to why it had been disturbed, perhaps even waiting for some gesture of dismissal.

I had an affair many years ago with a girl called Deidre. It was one of those sultry affairs, passionate but full of unease and uncertaintly. One evening I was waiting for Deidre in a coffee shop on the North Circular Road just a few streets from the Psychiatric Hospital where she worked. It was the same place in which we usually met. In fact our evenings together were entirely predictable, in an unpredictable sort of way; it was as if we were acting out a drama for which the scenario had been written already, yet each performance being live, generated its own tensions and its own suspense — hence that feeling of uncertainty I mentioned. As a man of the world, you will understand exactly what I mean. You too have often been racked by the same dilemma: Will she? Won't she? At my place? At hers? In the end she always did, but not until I was stretched to a fibre with expectancy. And yet she wasn't the tantalising type, definitely not that type. I think her uncertainty may have been the result of an inward struggle against the voluptuousness of her own nature. The struggle was pointless, as she always came to realise, eventually, thankfully.

But this particular evening was to be different, very different. I waited for her in that deserted cafe, sitting among formica tables under garish Italian tourist-posters, breathing-in the steamy odour of pasta, planning my seduction strategy, indulging in lustful thoughts.

When she arrived I was immediately struck by the seriousness of her expression: her face was slightly drawn, her eyes meditative. It was disconcerting. Her habitual mood was one of gaiety and joy; she was almost profligate in the diffusion of her emotional warmth. Furthermore, her mood was buoyant; never before had I seen that bright face of hers totally submerged in the gloom of the moment. What could be the matter?

She sat down at my table, opposite me, and ordered a coffee from the waiter who had ambled over after her.

'Hello,' I greeted her probingly.

'Hello,' she responded with the momentary flash of a smile evocative of a faint sunburst through a bank of dark cloud.

'Did you have a difficult day?'

'It was dreadful.'

I knew that she was working in the ward where they kept the most disturbed patients. She never talked about her work, but I had often suspected that she found some of her experiences harrowing.

'Where would you like to go? I have tickets for the cinema, the International, but if you're not in the humour we need not go. We can go to a disco instead.'

'No, the cinema is fine. Which film?'

'Onibaba.'

'Oney what?'

' "Onibaba" It's Japanese. I think it means "The Hole".'

'Not another one of those,' she replied with mock-weariness in her voice, yet again with the slight hint of a smile. She was referring, of course, to a current penchant of mine for Japanese films. There had been a stream of them flowing into the city in those days — it was the heyday of Shindo, and Shinoda, and Kurosawa — and I never permitted one to drift away again without having seen it. So the unfortunate Deidre (or Mary, or Ann, for that matter) was dragged along to witness Samurai massacres, and battles, and harakiris. The only relieving factor was that she often missed gory scenes because she was preoccupied trying to keep abreast of the sub-titles.

Nevertheless, I was anxious about bringing Deirdre to see that film on that particular night, because of her evidently low spirits. She was insistent that we go, however, and there was absolutely no putting her off.

You are quite familiar with the film, so you will understand immediately that it was not the best choice of entertainment for a girl whose nerves were raw. I was surprised that she survived those early scenes where the Samurai warriors fall to their death down the hole which the two women had so cunnigly contrived as a trap. Oddly, it was at that comical but bizarre scene where Toshiro Milfune runs through the long grass almost crazed by his sexual frustration, that she first began to waver. And while Mifune rolled and roared in frenzy, poor Deirdre grabbed my arm and buried her forehead in my shoulder. I sensed something of the depths of her nausea, the gush supressed behind clenched teeth. Taking her hand as gently as I could, I led her out of the cinema.

She did not want to go to a restaurant or a bar, so I brought her back to my flat. There I put a match to the fire I had ready-made in the grate and opened a bottle of Spanish wine. Soothed by the soft firelight and the sweet wine, Deirdre began to recover. We sat on the carpet, close to one another, our backs resting against the side of an armchair. In hesitating phrases and long intervals of silence she started to explain what had upset her.

Working in her ward of disturbed patients that morning, she had gone with another nurse to carry out a routine check on a patient in one of the padded cells. He was prone to violent fits, but his aggression was never directed against other people, so they had no worries about entering his cell. When Deirdre peeped through the door she found him lying quietly in his bed. She entered the room casually with her colleague, and they began their inspection. Immediately, something caught Deirdre's eye. It was a blotch of red blood seeping upwards through the white sheet that covered the patient. For a moment she was shocked. She glanced at the man's face. He was staring at the ceiling, engrossed, as if he

were unaware of their presence. And on his face, Deirdre
said, there was the strangest expression she had ever seen, an
expression of total serenity, utter calm, absolute peace. She
quickly snapped back the sheet. What she beheld she described in monosyllables, holding her face in the palms of her
hands in an effort to repress the nausea that kept welling-up
inside her, threatening to spill over at any moment. The
man's groin and stomach were a mass of blood and raw flesh.
His hands too were bloody. At first glance it looked like
widespread self-mutilation. But when she examined him
closely, it became clear what had happened: the man had
castrated himself with his bare hands; with his own fingernails
he had thorn out his testicles. Can you imagine? Deirdre told
me that she saw wads of flesh-tissue still lodged under his
nails.

Was it any wonder that the poor girl had recoiled from the
image of Mifune ranting and raving frenziedly in the long
grass? I was shocked on hearing her account of the incident;
how much more shocking it must have been for her who had
experienced it.

Deirdre slept in my arms that night, but any thought of
sexuality between us would have been unconscionable. Never
before had I seen the girl so defenceless, so vulnerable, so
passive. In that, possibly, lay the reason why I did not wish
to press home an advantage. Or maybe I had lost all appetite
for sex after listening to her account of that gruesome
incident. I was certainly unmanned by it. Lying there, wide
awake, with Deirdre's soft body close to me, I could not
wrench my mind off the lunatic who had castrated himself
with his bare hands. One detail of Deirdre's description had
particularly fascinated me, the unearthly expression of peace
on the man's face. It had even puzzled Deirdre. Did he feel
that a lifetime of torment was over? Or was there any coher-
ent thought in his mind? That calm, that serenity was exasper-
ating, as if, somewhere far beyond the frontiers of rational
thought, he had driven a salient into the bulwarks of ultimate
wisdom. It vexed me deeply, because, even though I could
not understand his state of mind, a bothersome intuition
kept insinuating that his was the condition of every man,
that, if there was a difference between the torture that had

driven this lunatic to pluck out his testicles and the torture of any ordinary man suffering the anguish of hopeless love for a woman, it was a difference of degree and not of kind. That same lunatic might have been burning with a passion for the girl next door, or for a secretary at his office, or even for one of his nurses. What if he had been in love with Deirdre?

I looked at her sleeping innocently in the crook of my arm. Never did I feel so close to her before. This closeness was partly, if not totally, due to the abandonment of sexuality. Of that I am certain. That presence, which had chaperoned my relationship with her up until then, which by turns had acted as buffer and plaything and go-between, was for the first time absent, banished by a madman lying mutilated in the lunatic asylum, and I found myself alone with my girl for the very first time; united in the sympathy and innocence of that moment, she was to me a sister more than a mistress.

That is the experience. I tell it to you as precisely as I can recall it, and I leave you to draw your own conclusions, if you are so inclined. But beware — they were very special circumstances and it might be dangerous to make a generalisation based on them.

Eternal Navvy

Christmas Eve. High-pitched voices coming from the canteen further down the corridor. Singing, bragging, telling jokes. Neon-tubes were a cold reminder of the fairy-lights brightening the houses with unreal colour back on Earth. In front of him one of the tubes flickered feebly at half-illumination. How dirty it was. Nobody cleaning lamp-shades here.

Jim Maguire waited in a queue outside the videophone box. Only one box in the whole of Bubble 314. It was a bloody disgrace. Five men in front of him. He checked his watch. 19.50.

Bubble 314 was a unit of the Moon Development Project, the 3 indicating that it belonged to the third complex — on the Sea of Serenity. 'Bubble' was what the men called each unit, because of the dome overhead which contained the simulated atmosphere. The twenty domes of Complex 3 presented a weird aspect, particularly when seen from overhead, as they stood out in stark contrast to the craters which pock-marked the surrounding landscape. 'Looks like a bloody Aero Bar.' Jim recalled the remark of one man as their spacecraft hovered over the landing-pad. 'Looks more like a witch's cauldron'. replied someone else.

The noise from the canteen was getting louder, more boisterous. Dozens of migrant labourers trying to convince themselves that it was Christmas Eve. Perhaps they were trying to forget it was Christmas Eve.

Jim didn't go drinking when he came off shift at 17.30. Instead, he went back to his cubicle, washed, shaved, and put on his best clothes. He wanted to be looking well. She was going to bring the children. A special treat for Christmas. He couldn't afford many videophone calls. This one was going to cost him a full week's wages.

He had told her to expect his call between 20.00 and 21.00. But would she find the box vacant? She would have to drive into Crossboher, and there was only one videophone box there, in the Post Office. If there were many people making calls from it he might have difficulty getting through.

An elevator down the corridor discharged a group of workers coming off their shift in the mine. Straight for the canteen, without washing faces, without changing clothes. Loud shouts greeted them as they went through the door.

The box was vacated and the man at the top of the queue went in. Only four left.

This was probably the only time Jim would use the videophone. He was on a two-year contract and had almost completed one year. February twelve-months he would be going home. It was, of course, lonely being so far from home. But the money was good. Even better money to be had on the new project just opened on Mars, but Jim had no inclination to go that far. Besides, a new project like that would be dangerous.

The Moon was quite safe now. Seldom any mishaps. In fact, they were even building a housing complex to accommodate workers' families. Jim had been offered a flat, but he had declined. No place to bring up kids. And it would have meant signing up for at least five years. Still, many of the Irish workers were opting for the flats. They felt it was no worse than Birmingham or Glasgow, or Frankfurt. And maybe they were right.

But Jim intended to keep his family at home in Crossboher. He was going to have a new house built when he returned. The Building Corporation's catalogue of house plans was his constant study. He had picked out the model he wanted, and he would have enough money saved from his wages to pay for it. Then, if the bonuses were good, he might be able to live at home for a year before having to go on another contract.

Box vacated, box occupied again. Three left. A puff of air in the corridor indicated the arrival of the elevator. Littered papers fluttered a little, then settled down over the dust-drifts that had blown into corners. Three black workers got out of

the elevator and walked off in the direction of the dormitor-
ies. No shift going on now. For two days the mine would be
manned by safety and security personnel only. No digging
over Christmas.

The man who had gone into the box put his head out
through the door. 'Damn channel seems to be jammed.'

The second man in the queue stuck his head in to have a
look. He twisted some of the knobs, slapped the screen a
few times with open hand. Shook his head. No luck.

'Probably overloaded. Everyone is trying to get through
tonight. I'll fetch the service engineer. He might be able to
get the line clear, if he's sober.'

'These damn things never work when you want them to,'
said the man in the box with disgust. 'I bet the four over in
the White-Collar Unit are working all right, though.'

Jim glanced at his watch again. 20.25. She would wait for
a while, in case he was just delayed getting through.

The service engineer arrived. No traces of intoxication. He
inserted a key and opened back a huge panel to reveal the
entrails of the machine. He checked about twenty points,
made adjustments here and there, closed the panel, looked at
the screen, shook his head. No use. Too many homesick
migrants jamming up the channels.

'It will probably clear in a couple of hours,' said the engineer. He gathered up his kit and left.

20.45. No hope of getting the call through now. He'd have
to ring later on the telephone. She'd be back in the house at
22.00 or 22.30.

Jim folded the newspaper he had been scanning and listened once more to the sounds from the canteen. Then he turned abruptly. To hell with the drink. He didn't feel like drinking. Quite depressed in fact. Disappointed for the kids'
disappointment. Disappointed for his own disappointment,
too. He had been looking forward to seeing them. Changed,
they would be changed. Now he would have to wait until the
day after Stephen's Day when the Post Office in Crossboher
opened again. Bloody machines. They never work when you
need them.

Queen B

for John F. Deane

Monday was his name, because Monday was his day. Monday was a B, a very disgruntled worker B. Drudging and monotonous his life, his future appeared equally dreary and unpromising.

Sunday night in the grey and cheerless dormitory, Monday was now top of the queue. He was in the first bunk, and the other five were occupied by the worker Bs in chronological order down to the far end where the spry figure of veteran Saturday hardly sagged the final bunk. Sunday, of course, fat voluptuary, was not there; it was his night in the chamber of the Queen B.

For Monday the craving had been building up from the middle of the week and was now at its most intense. Waking or asleep he had no escape; racked between repulsion and attraction, he dreamt of delectable disgusting honey of generation oozing in dewy beads among black hairs on soft flesh. Spurred by his fierce desire he would rise at dawn the following day and labour unceasingly in his allotment, gathering the succulent stems of the wild scutch grass and the petals of the crimson poppies. At sunset he would take up his bundle and carry it to the chamber of the Queen B. As usual, she would mutter and grumble while she rummaged and nibbled, with never a pleasant word of gratitude and never a compliment. But when she was sated with food she would lie back on her couch and slowly raise her arm to expose — o heaven, o hell — her armpit, his personal armpit, with black hairs on soft flesh, and o, the bitter-sweet syrup of oblivion beckoning to him in beads of crystalline sweetness. And he would creep up, for how could he resist! And with his tongue he would lap the fullness of her secretion, suck the luscious loathsome honey of generation, assuager of all torments, balm of all sores, sedative of all anxious thoughts. For the whole night he would lie oblivious in the bed of that armpit, all pain, all depression suspended, until the first cold trickle of grey reality filtred into the chamber. Then the arm of the Queen B would be lowered, like a surly portcullis, and the armpit, his armpit, folded away for another week. With no more ceremony than when he arrived, and with less display of emotion, he would depart.

The days of the week were seven, because the armpits of the Queen B were seven; and the number of weeks in the month was four because every fourth week the Queen B laid her clutch of eggs.

Sitting on the edge of his bunk, using several of his long black arms in the exercise, Monday aimlessly rotated a metal disk which he had found in his allotment. He was brooding, as he frequently was, on the emptiness of his existence, the pointlessness of his drudgery, and the relentless craving which enslaved him to his treadmill. Every week he thought of leaving. But, just as often he failed to overcome his dependence on that one night of oblivion; just as often he flinched at the prospect of a future without the occasional obliteration of consciousness. Once, he tried to rebel against the indignity of his situation by refusing to go to the chamber of the Queen B on his appointed night. Defiant, resolute, he lay in his bunk. The other workers surrounded him and begged him not to upset the blessed pattern of domestic order. Monday was unmoved. They threatened to break one of his arms, so that he would no longer be able to maintain his position in the Queen's household, but would be dragged to the frontiers of the domain and flung over the boundary wall to fend for himself among the hungry nomad Bs in the wilderness beyond. He was not daunted. Then Thursday, the oldest of the seven workers, explained that if Monday refused to go that night, then Tuesday would become Monday. That convinced him. Life was bad enough. His grasp on time and place was feeble enough without losing whatever semblance of identity he already possessed. He could not suffer the humil-

iation of having to become Tuesday or Wednesday. He yield-
ed. Picking up his ignominious bundle he proceeded to the
Queen's chamber and entered with apologies and excuses for
his unpunctuality.

The weeks and months rolled by, as nature had ordained.
Every month a new batch of eggs was laid, fertilised by the
white dust of procreation falling from the whisker of the
worker as he lapped the honey of generation. Ceremoniously
the eggs were borne to the boundary wall of the domain, and
there dumped unceremoniously into the wilderness to perish
or survive as chance should determine. And the whole cycle
seemed to Monday as pointless as it was interminable.

Slowly and decisively, Monday stopped rotating the metal
disk. Using a sharp corner of the bunk-frame, he scratched
the word NO into its polished surface. He then scooped out
a hole in the ground, buried the disk, and covered it over.

With the same deliberate motion he passed down through
the dormitory for the last time and out the exit door. Outside
he paused for a moment and glanced around and up at the
great dome of the heavens. What a wide place the world was,
now that he experienced the freedom to explore it!

> *North, south, east, or west,*
> *Which direction will I find best?*

He picked the east, fixed his eye upon a hill afar off in that
direction, and hurried towards it as quickly as his skelter of
legs could carry him.

As he approached the boundary wall he was conscious of
an array of beady eyes glinting in the wilderness, peering at
him, observing his course, hungry eyes that would scour the
seven allotments of the domain in the first light of dawn to
confirm his going. And then the ritual of challenge and com-
bat would be initiated to determine who would take his place;
he who succeeded in killing or maiming all his rivals would
step into the domain before evening to claim his prize.
Monday would have liked to stay and watch the contest; he
would even have liked to loiter long enough to see the
warrior emasculated by that same prize. But he dared not.
The craving was too strong. He had to keep moving, to put as

wide a buffer as he could between himself and the object of his craving.

And as he passed through the night he heard the buzz of coversation from the encampments of the nomads, and the sweet whistle of the ilka-bird. He jogged to the rhythm of the brooks, and somersaulted in delight at the sight of a tumbling star.

By the time daylight came, Monday was far away from the domain, among new hills and strange meadows. He felt that he had now distanced himself sufficiently from the location of his former way-of-life to have broken its hold. Down in the grass he lay and slept lightly and happily for a long long while.

When he woke up, the crisp yellow sun was high in the heavens; a warm breeze redolent of shrubs and flowers came rolling over the plain; and the timber boughs of the tree-tops reverberated the music of birdsong. Truly this was a new birth, in unimagined and unimaginable contrast to his former existence.

Down the meadow, Monday saw the most beautiful sight he had ever seen, a princess B passing over the earth with a grace that left him breathless. He hurried down to observe her from a closer vantage point. In her path the buttercups bowed their heads in deference to her more exquisite loveliness. She was at that most beautiful time of life, fully grown, on the verge of maturity, soon to be a queen, yet retaining all the vernal innocence of youth.

Monday was following her, automatically, unconsciously, when she stopped, turned around, and faced him. It was an embarrassing moment for Monday, who stopped dead and stared at her. But she smiled at him, and radiated a beam of such warm vibrations that his embarrassment melted away; the limits of his isolation quite dissolved, and the darkest corner of his spirit was illuminated. He responded out of the growing fullness of his warmth and light, transmitted similar rays through the prisms of his shining eyes, until either soul basked in the other's radiance. And the most wonderful thing of all, to Monday, was the fact that this absolute mutual understanding, this profound emotional exchange, happened instantaneously, unadulterated by the profanity of sound or touch.

She turned, as if in total confidence that the ecstasy would last. He followed. Their movement was a joyful dance, like the bucking of the first lamb of spring, full of the newness of the world, full of the wonder of experience freshly felt.

And for a month, Monday gladly followed the graceful movements of the Princess B. Loth was he to take his eyes off her, even for the fraction of a moment; nothing could entice him from her presence, even for the fraction of a fraction of a moment. In brief intervals of reflection, Monday realised that he had been completely shrived of all his lustful cravings. Indeed he had almost forgotten his life with the Queen B, until a raw and jealous wind blowing from the bitter north whispered in his ear that the Princess herself would soon be a queen. The image of his beloved Princess transformed into an ugly bloated female horrified poor Monday. Out of his despair he cried aloud to the trees:

> O, how shall I
> Stop
> The trickle
> > of the sands
> > > of time?
> How?
> O, how shall I
> Protect
> My darling
> > from the fate-rot
> > > of ripeness?
> How?
> O, how?

And the oak, the oldest and the wisest of the trees, answered him in a low and measured monotone. He told Monday that there was one antidote to the fate-rot of ripeness: the Princess would have to eat the berries of the magic rowan which grew on top of the highest peak of the mountain; she would have to eat the fruit of the tree of imagination.

Monday was so relieved, so overjoyed, that he tumbled the wildcat clear across the meadows. The Princess followed him, smiling indulgently at his display of excessive delight. Then he led her directly to the slopes of the mountain, and they began the long climb towards the highest peak.

Long they dallied on the lower slopes and frolicked among the blossoms of the purple heather. Long they dawdled with the mountain rabbits and sprawled in unconcern upon the banks of quickly moving streams. Then, beset by anxious thoughts, they would strive for a long while and move further and further up the mountain slopes.

They reached the base of the highest peak. The sun was shining; the sky was blue; and the air was clear. They lay down to admire the great spread of the landscape stretched out before them. Not a puff of wind was blowing to cool away the heat of their endeavours. The Princess reclined with her graceful black arms behind her on the rising ground. Monday was below her, gazing fondly up at her.

It was then that he noticed it. Horror of all horrors! Too late they were, too late in reaching the tree of imagination. The process of maturation had begun; the rot had already started to take its course. Glistening in the sunlight that shone down on her exposed armpits, Monday beheld honey-beads swelling to succulent ripeness, heaven and hell materialising before his eyes. Transfixed, powerless, he shuddered with pain and ecstasy. His lustful hunger, like a river that had been building up behind a dam, fell upon him with a hundred times its original force.

He did what he had to do. He crept up to her, embraced her, and with his tongue in her delicious armpit he lapped the honey of generation, opium of workers, syrup of dreams. For seven days and seven nights they lay embraced at the foot of the peak, Monday devouring the first fruits of the Princess's abundant harvest. From one armpit to the other he went, tasting bliss in the soft fold of each, until finally the week was spent.

After the seventh day the Princess arose and stood a little way off. She was changed. Now she was a queen. For a little while she remained motionless and self-absorbed, as if she were trying to come to terms with the metamorphosis. When she eventually began to move she did so without any reference to Monday; without turning towards him, she began the journey down the mountain. He followed, a little way behind, no longer equal — dependent, addicted, manacled.

When they reached the level ground the Queen did not stop; she continued on, commencing the quest for a suitable domain. Far and wide she ranged. Monday took no part in the search; he merely followed where she led. The Queen had now assumed absolute responsibility, her self-importance swelling like the eggs in her ovary, and Monday was reduced to the status of an appendage.

At length they came to a domain which, from all appearances, had only recently been vacated; the structures of the buildings were still intact and the seven allotments still neatly divided. The death of its former queen was the probable explanation why it had been forsaken and yet left in such an excellent state of repair. The Queen took possession of the quarters appropriate to her, and Monday retired to the dormitory of the workers.

Already there was a massing at the boundary and a contest imminent to decide who should occupy the other six positions.

Monday found the dormitory to be cheerless and grey, exactly like the previous one he had known; the bunks here too were laid out in a neat file, six of them. He went up slowly to the first bunk and sat down on it. Drained by despair, he felt a sense of the utter impossibility of freedom. His eyes bent on the beaten clay of the floor. In front of him he noticed a little patch where the clay was looser than anywhere else. Impelled by a vague recollection, he quickly dug into that patch, his many hands working through the soft clay with impetuous speed. Presently he struck, what he suspected he might find, a shining metal disk. Taking it up and rubbing off the dirt he was able to read the letters scraped boldly on to its surface, 'NO'.

Three for Oblivion

They were the oddest group I ever picked up since I started working the Lethe crossing. Three of them there were, so separate yet so similar, so wrapped up in the rags of their self-importance. They were loitering on the pier — where I picked you up just now — holding their backs towards one another, trying to pretend that their journeys would never overlap, that their destinations could not possibly coincide. I may as well admit that I do not understand your fellow-countrymen; but I find them amusing, and intriguing. Yes indeed, they never cease to intrigue me.

The charred remains of their clothing were ripped and shredded, rendering the three men indistinguishable one from another were it not for the spectacular exception of their ties. Whatever catastrophe had sent them here together had evidently been powerless to bleach the colour from those strange pendants which hung loosely, noose-like, about their necks.

When I pulled the boat up to the pier they boarded so silently, so sullenly, so formally, you'd think they were in the regular unpleasant habit of catching the ferry. Sullen as they were, I was glad of the business, for business does not often come my way. Indeed what could be more futile than the occupation of the Ferryman on Lethe? Old Charon, up on Styx, has a fine time by comparison: he gets the full stream of traffic entering the Underworld, and he gets it first: by the time he relieves them of their coins there is nothing left for the rest of us — as if Styx were the only river they might want to cross. But I believe that even Charon is complaining lately. They come as penniless as paupers, expecting to be ferried over for nothing, you'd think it was a social service we were running instead of a business. O yes, and I've heard that some of these fly-boys are pulling the wool over poor old Charon's eyes, cutting the shiny buttons off their habits and passing them off as coins. And you've seen Charon: you know how old and doddery and blind he is; he can't keep up with all the changes in currencies and thinks the buttons are minted by some of these new countries which send us so much business nowadays. But don't get me wrong — I'm not sorry for the old bag: he has his fortune made and should have retired long ago. It's the attitude to authority I deplore. No respect. They have absolutely no respect for authority.

As bad as things are for Charon, they're far worse for me here on Lethe. Those who journey this far do not come to catch the ferry. They bathe in the river, and take the waters; occasionally they swim across. I suppose you could describe this as the spa of the Underworld; although, if you want my opinion, that treacle-black slurry is far less inviting than a sulphur bath. But it has its qualities, I'll admit, and its cure is guaranteed! They come from all over, you know -- the ones that want to forget, the ones that are burdened with guilt, the ones with the dark secrets — and look, see how thirstily they swarm around the waters. I must tell you a phrase, coined by a former passenger, to describe that scene; a very disdainful gentleman, but generous, very generous, he was viewing the scene from that same seat in which you are now sitting; he turned scornfully to me and said, 'wouldn't they remind you of flies around a shite.' An excellent analogy, don't you think?

Now you realise what a ridiculous job I have, providing a ferry service on Lethe, waiting for the occasional passenger to make his way on to the pier. You can also imagine how happy I was to pick up the three Irishmen together, even though one glance revealed that they carried not so much as a can of paint for the sodden timbers of my old craft.

I pushed off from the pier and rowed out into the stream, bearing an open mind as to the course I should take with my passengers. You will understand that, if they had naught to pay their passage, I was perfectly entitled to dump them overboard and let them swim to shore minus their precious memories. On the other hand, I should mention that I am very liberal as to the form of payment. I am prepared to accept any trifle. Indeed, I regard even an interesting conversation or a humorous anecdote as a tolerable reward for my labours. Those alone I abominate who make no offer whatsoever, either by way of goods or by way of conversation.

When I reached midstream I eased up on the oars and let the boat drift idly with the current, just like this. For a while they paid no heed; they were probably trying to convince themselves that the situation was normal. Eventually the silence grew tense and shuffling, until it was broken by an outburst from the one I shall call Green Tie, for want of any other method of identification.

'Hey, mister, is this your coffee break or something? Why don't you lean on those pins? I can't stay floating around on this bleedin' pond forever, you know.'

'We shall resume our journey as soon as you meet your obligations,' I replied.

'What do you mean?' he snarled defensively.

'You haven't yet offered to pay your fare,' said I.

'Look, mister, if that's your idea of a joke, then I'm laughing, laughing like hell - HA -HA -HA - sorry if I don't sound amused. Now you can get on with the job like a good man.'

'I am not joking. You have taken the ferry; you must pay your fare. Surely that is not an unreasonable request.'

'You know damned well that I have no money to pay fares.'

'Then you shouldn't have taken the ferry,' said I, lifting the oars out of the rowlocks. 'But I am in no hurry. I can wait until the three of you decide to pay your way, if you should wish to proceed farther.'

'This is ridiculous,' took up White Tie. 'I thought that, coming down here, I would at least have no more worries about transport strikes.'

'I lived in a high-rise block in Belfast,' stated Orange Tie, 'and I always had a dread of getting caught in the lift between floors. It never happened to me in Belfast; I had to come down here to get caught. It proves a lot of people wrong: Belfast is not worse than hell!'

Each and every remark was addressed directly at me, yet the realisation that they had been surprised into talking in each other's presence embarrassed them, and they fell silent once more. At length it was Green Tie whose restlessness got the better of him.

'Listen, mister. I'm giving you one last chance to get those oars moving. If you don't take that chance now, I'm going to relieve you of the oars. And you could get injured in the process.'

'Let me relieve you of any illusion you may have that you can resort to violence,' I replied calmly. 'Let me remind you of my somewhat superior station here. I may not be numbered with the gods but I do share something of their calibre.'

That took some of the wind from Green Tie. He sat back on the seat and stared sulkily out the starboard side. Another long interval of silence followed.

'If you won't row us over,' faltered White Tie, 'perhaps you wouldn't mind bringing us back to the jetty.'

'Cast your eyes towards either shore,' said I, 'and you will observe that it is as far to travel back as to travel forward. You may choose the shore of your destination, but either way you must pay the toll.'

'But I have nothing to offer you in payment,' wailed White Tie in desperation. 'So what option is open to me?'

'Why the obvious one, of course: you can swim to either shore.' I enjoyed watching the expression of horror that welled up into their three faces simultaneously.

'Not bleedin' likely,' declared Green Tie belligerently. 'And have every last thought flushed out of my brain. Not bleedin' likely.'

'The reason I took the ferry was to keep my memory intact,' said Orange Tie.

'What is so important about your particular memory?' I asked. 'Everyone else is driven by an anxious desire for amnesia. The waters of Lethe are regarded as the great consolation of the Underworld; why do you shun them as if they were poison?'

'Where I come from,' said Orange Tie in a tone of reminiscence, 'memory is sacred. It is as sacred to us as the tablets of stone were to the Jews; and the images engraved on our memory are just as durable as anything that was written on those same tablets. We remember what happened at the Boyne and on the walls of Derry. Those deeds are an example, a guide, a standard, a point of reference around which we mould our lives. Memory is the great storehouse of our tradition; it gives us identity and individuality; we would be nothing if our minds were not well fortified with memories of what our fathers and forefathers stood for and fought for.'

'What a restriction on your life your memory must have been,' I exclaimed. 'You should have tried to escape from it. You should have sought freedom; it would have been a higher aspiration.'

'Ach, no, that's nonsense. If it weren't for memory and tradition, what would mark me off from any Fenian; what would make me different from the Provo gett whose bomb sent me here?'

Green Tie shifted uneasily, aggressively.

'Memory is a wonderful thing,' sighed White Tie, anticipating a conflict between the other two. 'If it hadn't been for my childhood memories of the West of Ireland, I should have found life in the city unbearable. And I am sure that I could not now face the prospect of eternity without the succour of those same cherished memories.'

'I have discussed this subject with countless people on board this boat,' said I, 'and only one of them appeared to me to have a sensible reason for clinging to memory. He was a cynical rascal of a gentleman, but very generous. He maintained that his amorous exploits in the Upperworld were too good to be forgotten, and he was going to try and smuggle his memories of them into Elyzium. I wouldn't have given much for his chances, although, on the other hand, I wouldn't be surprised if he succeeded; he was a resourceful scoundrel and had a way with people.'

'What do you think of our chances of getting into Elyzium?' asked White Tie.

'I think there is very little possibility of that. People nowadays have such misconceptions, it never ceases to amaze me. They think that, if they have done nothing wrong, they have lived a good life and, so, should qualify for admission to Elyzium. It isn't like that at all. On being born into the Upperworld a person is endowed with a potentiality for living. It is up to him to realise this potentiality, to live life fully and deeply, and thereby to develop his capacity for life. Without a highly developed capacity for life, a person is in an alien element when he gets to Elyzium, like a fish in the air, like a swallow at the bottom of the sea. There is a severe need for a prophet to go to the Upperworld and explain these things to them. Since the days of the Empire, people have gone very badly astray.'

'Do you mean the British Empire?' interjected Orange Tie hopefully.

'There was only one empire worthy of the name, the Roman Empire.' Orange Tie wilted in the glare of disgust that I could not help directing at him. 'None of you appears to me to have developed any capacity for living. For dying — yes. Your whole nation has developed an enormous capacity for death — as if death conferred value on anything. The sign of death is stamped on every frustrated impulse, every guilt-ridden joy, every achievement envy-maimed. You worship death with an idolatry far more fervent than that of any Dionysiac. You come to us with disease in your eyes, with decay in your hearts, with death in your still-born souls; and you have the arrogance to think that you are well-qualified for eternal life. No, my friends, you will not be admitted to Elyzium. If you are not consumed in your effrontery by the wrath of Jove, consider yourselves lucky. When you set foot on the Elysian shores you will, no doubt, be directed for re-cycling: all residue of conscious thought will be expunged from your minds and you will be sent back to the Upperworld with the opportunity of fulfilling at least one of the potentialities with which you will be endowed.'

'That doesn't sound so bad, but do they use any discretion as to where they send a person?' enquired Green Tie. 'Surely they would send a person back among his own people.'

'Where a person goes is a matter of absolute chance.'

'You mean that, if I go back, I might be born into a Loyalist house, and grow up a bleedin' Orangeman, ignorant as to who I really am.' Green tie sounded extremely worried.

'You might end up in the most unlikely place indeed. But how can you be so sure as to who you really are? You may have twenty lives over you already among different races and religions. So why should you regard your last one as more important than another?'

'I don't care what you say,' roared Green Tie. 'I'd rather

rot down here than risk going back up there as a Protestant. I have some patriotism left in me yet.'

'And I'm going to take no chance of going back as a Fenian and a Papist.' Orange Tie jumped to his feet and spat the words into the face of his fellow-passenger.

'Maybe we should turn around then and go back to the jetty.' White Tie got to his feet as well and stood between them to prevent a brawl. 'We don't have to go to Elyzium; millions before us have been content to remain in the teeming caverns of Hades. There, at least, we will have the comfort of our memories. For my part, I have no desire to be born again. If I were going back to the Upperworld, I would like to remember; I would like to see my children and my friends; I would like to visit the places I have loved. Otherwise, I see no purpose in going back.'

'What an enigma you are, the three of you: you find it so hard to live together; yet, you managed to die together. How did you contrive that?' I asked.

'We must have been caught in the same bomb-blast in Dublin.' replied White Tie.

'In Dublin!' gasped Green Tie. 'I must have forgotten. The fumes of this bleedin' river must be affecting me already. If it was in Dublin, then it must have been a Loyalist bomb.' He turned viciously on Orange Tie. 'I suppose it was your bomb, you licker of Britain's arse-hole.'

'Bugger-off, Napper Tandy. I'm proud to say that I have defended the Union, and I did whatever I was called on to do. But, to the best of my recollection, I was in Belfast when the bomb went off.'

'Come to think of it, I might have been in Belfast too. Yes, I was to go there on business. It's very hazy.' White Tie was racking his muddled brain — so much for his valued memory.

' I bet you were in Belfast,' exulted Orange Tie. 'And we know who was likely to be letting off bombs there. Don't we?'. He advanced menacingly on Green Tie. 'You Provo bastard, I'll bet it was you who pulled the gaff on the three of us.'

'Let there be no violence here,' shouted White Tie. 'It's this eternal hostility between the two of you that has put us in this predicament.'

'You keep out of this, you lush slob. You're probably a Provo sympathiser anyway.'

'I certainly am not a Provo sympathiser, and I have never condoned violence and murder. All civilised Irishmen believe that murder is a greater evil than any political arrangement of which we may disapprove. I include myself in that number and reject the use of violence as a means towards any end.'

'Oh really?' enquired Green Tie. 'Tell me this then: did you pay taxes when you were in your cushy job back in Dublin?'

Of course I did.'

'And those taxes were used to pay and equip an army. And that army was told to support the institutions of the state — by violent means if necessary. Look, brother, you believe in violence just like the rest of us, so don't be such a bleedin' hypocrite.'

'That's different,' cried White Tie indignantly.

'There's only one difference,' roared Green Tie. 'You hire your gunmen ; I carry the gun myself.'

'You were carrying the bomb that killed us, weren't you?' interjected Orange Tie. 'Admit it, you bastard.'

'I don't remember,' retorted Green Tie, squaring up to him, 'but I don't give a bleedin' curse whether I was or not.'

Genuinely worried that a fracas might overturn my boat, I roared at them, 'Sit down, the three of you, or you'll all end up in the river.' I handed my drinking cup to White Tie. 'Take a drink. It will cool you off.' He took the cup and looked at it, hesitating.

'Go on,' I said. 'It will do you a lot of good, and a single drink has no lasting effect on the memory.'

He leaned over the gunwhale and scooped a cupful of water impetuously from the river. But when he looked at the contents of the cup he was perceptibly shocked. For a few moments he continued staring into the cup. Then he smelt it, and tasted it.

'I don't believe it,' he gasped. 'It's stout, Guinness's stout, a whole river of it.' He turned his blank uncomprehending gaze out on the black expanse of Lethe.

The other two looked over his shoulder. Green Tie took the cup, smelt it and tasted it. 'It's bleedin' Guinness all right.

A riverful of draught stout!' cried he in ecstasy. 'I always knew that I'd go to heaven.'

'Where does this river rise? In a brewery?' Orange Tie addressed me, as he in turn took a sample from the cup. 'It's no wonder they're swarming around the banks.' He scooped another cupful from the river. 'Not a bad head on it either.' He pointed to the yellow froth he had managed to generate by the impetus of his hand.

The three of them sat back in the boat, passing the cup from one to another, admiring the froth, tasting the water — which they maintained was stout — comparing it to the brew served in taverns back in the Upperworld. Politics, religious divisions, violence, all such considerations faded quickly in the light of this new-found common interest. Around and around went the cup. They imbibed drink after drink. Presently, I knew they must be reaching the stage where the waters take their ordained effect, but I said nothing. Why should I try to stop them? After all, they were far more amenable, far more content. The change was undeniably for the better. There they were in the back of the boat, arms around one another, united as they had never been united before, attempting to sing:

> *And we'll all go together*
> *To pluck wild mountain thyme...*

Singing became progressively more difficult as the last residues of memorised data were expunged from their minds. Finally, unable to recall any more words, they fell inarticulate, and just continued humming and rocking to-and-fro to the rhythm they had already established.

I must confess that I was tempted by a cruel thought. To return and discharge them in their senseless, oblivious state on the pier where I had picked them up. Did they deserve any better? Come, be honest and frank; would it have been such an outrage to withdraw them from circulation? I think no-one would have condemned such an action; many might have applauded it. As usually happens, however, my generosity got the better of me. I addressed them as follows. I might as well have been talking to myself, of course, because they were now incapable of understanding a single word I said.

'Gentlemen, it is now of little moment whether you immerse yourselves in Lethe or not. But, since I undertook to ferry you across, I will complete the task. When you arrive on the Elysian shores you will be dispatched forthwith into a new life, and I hope you make more of your opportunities the next time around. Now, I always insist on payment, as a matter of principle; the only objects you appear to have that hold any interest to me are your ties; they have some colour, so I may be able to use them to decorate my boat. I will take your ties in payment of your fare. Agreed?'

They offered no objection, so I relieved them of their ties. As I resumed rowing towards Elyzium, they appeared to me the most pathetic of sights, huddled in the back seat, arms still entwined around one another. Without their ties they were now totally indistinguishable, and I could no longer recall who was who. Which of them was Green Tie, which Orange Tie? I had no way of making out. But what did it matter? I suspect they were far more similar to begin with than they would have been honest enough to admit.

I hung the three ties together from a pole on the stern. Have a look. Don't you think they look decorative? Green, white and orange. A curious combination of colours — but they do brighten up the drab outline of the boat.

You may have noticed that we have been drifting in midstream for quite a while now. I hate having to be blunt with people — it is not my style at all. But, since we left the pier, I have been hinting at it in the broadest possible manner: you have been sitting there without opening your mouth, without offering any token in payment of your fare.